Caroline's Purpose

Caroline's Purpose

Erica Zaborac

Torchflame Books

Durham, NC

Caroline's Purpose
Erica Zaborac
ericazaborac.wordpress.com
erica_zaborac@hotmail.com

Published 2021, by Torchflame Books
    an Imprint of Light Messages
www.lightmessages.com
Durham, NC 27713 USA
SAN: 920-9298

Paperback ISBN: 978-1-61153-392-7
E-book ISBN: 978-1-61153-393-4
Library of Congress Control Number: 2020922345

Mrs. Davenport,
thank you for helping me realize my dream in
fifth grade, and for being here
every step of the process.
Without you, none of this would be possible.

Also, in memory of my horse,
Bo (April 25, 1998-June 1, 2020).
Thank you for being my heart and inspiration.

One

THEY WERE FLYING. The tall green grass bowed in the breeze the horse and rider created as they passed. The trees and spectators were just a blur of color in their vision. Beau's hooves hardly spent any time on the ground as he galloped toward the next jump. Caroline saw the fence come into view and sat up, cueing her gelding to rebalance himself. He responded perfectly, listening to her body. Caroline smiled, loving the relationship the two shared, and how they could communicate without words.

The jump came closer and closer. Beau got his eyes and heart locked onto the jump. Caroline gave him one last half halt on the reins, then left him alone. They'd be in the air in three...two...one...

Caroline sat up in the dark with a shock, her t-shirt clinging to her damp skin. It took her a moment to remember where she was. She wasn't on Beau galloping around the cross-country course. She was in her bed, in her room, tangled in sheets from tossing and turning. The now-familiar ache in her right elbow brought her back to the present even more. She reached for her phone to check the time, seeing it was just after three in the morning.

She kicked herself free from the sheets, so she could dry off. Her heart was still racing. She laid her hands across her face and forced her breathing to slow down. Tears of frustration stung her eyes. She wiped them away with a quick, closed fist.

Caroline knew going back to sleep wouldn't be possible after that dream. She climbed out of bed and padded across the soft carpet to her desk. She rolled the chair out and plopped down. She twisted the knob of her lamp, sighing as the light reflected on the shiny new textbooks lying in front of her. The first classes of her sophomore year of college would begin later that day.

She ran her fingers over the cover of the top book, the one for her general chemistry class. The cover creaked as she opened it. She flipped through the pages, eyeing the graphs and charts and the periodic table, wondering how she would ever be able to understand the concepts.

Caroline closed the chemistry book and glanced at the covers of the texts for her other classes. It was going to be a tough semester with economics and statistics on top of chemistry. But those weren't the classes she was dreading the most.

Along with the academically challenging classes, she also found herself taking Intro to Horse Science, and Weanling Training and Management, courses she wasn't sure she could handle. The idea of being around horses again was causing her nightmares, when she could fall asleep at all.

She hadn't enrolled in those classes by choice. Her academic advisor had been pushing her to choose a major, and because of her past, had suggested Equine Science. Caroline's throat had closed, and she hadn't been able to say no. She hadn't been able to say anything. Her advisor didn't know why she had left the horse world all behind her.

Very few people knew.

Caroline set the textbooks aside and reached for her laptop. If she couldn't sleep, she could at least get organized for the semester. She logged in to the University of Arizona website and grabbed her planner. She went class by class, syllabus by syllabus, until every homework assignment, project, and test were written in and highlighted in her calendar. At least she could control those kinds of details.

She was still wide awake when she finished with the last class. Closing her laptop, she scooted her chair away from the desk. She thought about how much more time she would have to study this semester, since she had lost her roster spot on the softball team due to an injury. She still had a managerial position with the team, but that wouldn't be as time consuming as being an athlete. She spun the chair back and forth, taking in the bare, lavender-painted walls staring back at her.

She had torn all the pictures and plaques from the walls two months ago, when she was told she would never play softball again. The glimmer of the overhead lights on the trophies and medals and the smiles of her teammates had been almost as painful as the torn tendon in her elbow. She couldn't fix her own arm, but she could get rid of everything that reminded her of her love for the game, of her success on the field. Of everything she had lost. It was all stuffed into a couple of boxes and hidden away in the back of her closet. Another former life, another set of painful memories, packed away and out of her sight. If only it was that simple to get them out of her heart.

Caroline blinked and pushed herself up out of the chair and back to her bed, clicking off the lamp as she went. She needed to try to rest so she wouldn't be useless on her first day of classes. Watching the ceiling fan spin above her head, counting its rotations, she tried to stop her mind from racing. Her eyes moved from the fan to the dresser, where her dust-covered Bible sat. For a moment, she considered getting up and opening it, as reading the words had once been enough to help her breathe and relax. To find peace and purpose. But not anymore. God had taken away everything good in her life. There was no point in opening the book. Caroline rolled over to her side and pulled her blanket over her head.

It felt like only minutes had passed when her heart skipped a beat and she jumped as the alarm on her phone started screeching at her. Reaching far to her left, she used her thumb to stop the noise.

Her feet scuffled across the carpet as she dragged them to the bathroom. The mint of her toothpaste mixed with the salt of a few stray tears that dripped down her cheeks and into her mouth. She scrubbed away the trails they left, drying her eyes before putting on mascara.

The dresser drawer creaked when she opened it. She grabbed a polo and a pair of shorts, pulling them on without looking at her reflection...without letting her tired eyes find the school logo or the script spelling out *softball* underneath it. She reached for her gym bag and put in a pair of rough, worn jeans before going to her closet to find her old paddock boots. She hadn't touched them in years, and a thin layer of arena dirt and hay still covered them. She stuffed them in with the jeans and zipped the bag shut. After slamming her books into her backpack, she threw the pack over her shoulder, crumpled the gym bag in her fist, and headed to the kitchen for breakfast.

Her dad stood over the stove, sizzling bacon and flipping pancakes. She dropped her bags by the front door and sat down on the stool by the counter.

"Morning, kiddo. This'll be ready in just a second.

How'd you sleep?" Doug Davis's six-foot, two-inch athletic frame towered over the burner as he adjusted the temperature. Even though it had been years since his last game, the muscles in his right arm still showed how dominate of a major league baseball pitcher he had been.

"I slept fine," Caroline lied. "Where's Mom?"

"She had an early lesson to teach, so she's outside already." He dished Caroline's breakfast on to a plate. "She said to tell you to have a good day."

Caroline nodded her head as she poured syrup over her pancakes. Her mom, Holly, worked as a horse trainer and was still one of the top three-day eventers in the country. Her parents were very different and had separate passions, but they were a perfect match. Together, they made their farm the high-class facility it was.

Because of each of their interests, Caroline had been encouraged to pursue both softball and eventing. She had done very well in each sport, but now, because of fate's awful sense of humor, she had lost both.

"You okay over there?" Her dad interrupted her thoughts.

"Yeah, I'm good." Caroline scooped a bite of pancakes into her mouth.

"Seemed like you were somewhere else there. Worried about the semester?"

"A little, but I'm sure it'll be fine."

"Econ and stats won't be as bad as you're thinking. You're smart. I'm sure you'll figure it out." Doug smiled and winked.

Caroline swallowed. "Thanks, Dad."

"Anytime."

Caroline finished her breakfast and checked the time on her Fitbit. "I better get going." She stood and put her plate in the sink. Stooping down, she gathered her things, patting the front of her backpack to check for her keys and wallet.

"What's in your gym bag? Are you gonna work out with the team?" Her dad peeked his head around the corner toward the front door.

Caroline's heart stopped, and panic caused her stomach to tense. "Um, yeah," she mumbled. "I thought I would run with them if I had time. You know, relieve some stress."

"Sounds like a good idea to me. Enjoy your first day, kiddo." He turned back to the kitchen.

"I'm sure I will." She opened the door and headed for her car, glancing down the driveway toward the barn and the arenas. She saw her mom standing in the middle of the dressage arena, teaching a lady on a light gray horse. Her mom was so focused on the lesson, she didn't notice Caroline standing there watching. Tearing her eyes free from the scene in front of her, Caroline opened her car door and got in, putting her bags in the passenger seat. Her gaze fixed onto her gym bag, forcing her to think about the lie she had just told her dad.

She hadn't told either of her parents about the Equine classes she was taking, and she didn't plan to. Better to keep them in the dark and not get their hopes up that she was returning to the horse scene. She felt guilty about keeping it a secret, and even guiltier about lying, but there was nothing else she could do. Her decision had been made. There would be no going back. With one last glimpse toward her mom in the arena, and a sigh that lifted her blond bangs off her forehead, she put her car in reverse and pulled away from the house, dragging herself toward reality.

Two

CONNOR TAYLOR PULLED HIS TRUCK into the grassy parking area at the University of Arizona Equine Center and cut the engine. He stared in awe at the pastures that stretched out in front of him. Most of them were filled with ten to fifteen horses, all with their muzzles down to the grass, grazing in the green oasis that was somehow located in the middle of the Tucson desert. Ten weanlings crowded the nearby pasture fence, eyeing his truck with cautious suspicion. Connor pried open his door, creating just enough space for him to slide out from behind the steering wheel, not wanting to startle them.

One of the babies nickered as Connor stepped toward the enclosure. The young horse pushed his way through the herd, eyeing Connor. Bigger than the other foals, his coat shone like copper. A wide white stripe blazed down the center of his face.

"Hi, buddy." Connor reached through the fence as the colt stretched his head and neck toward Connor's hand. "You must be in charge out here the way you just plowed your way over everybody." The horse bobbed his head up and down, as if he was nodding in agreement.

Connor studied the rest of the weanlings, estimating their ages and breeding with the skills he had gained from growing up on his parents' breeding farm. The large colt who had nickered at him was probably the oldest, close to six months old. The smallest filly in the group looked to be between three and four months old. All of their coats glittered in the warm sunshine. Their developing muscles rippled as they moved, showing the talented athletes they would grow up to be. They were all stunning. If God made something more beautiful, He had kept it for Himself.

Lord, thank You for creating these creatures and for giving me this opportunity. I'm really looking forward to this class and this program.

A light breeze blew across the pasture, ruffling the manes and tails of the horses in front of him. Other cars began pulling into the lot, and the group of babies went to see each person as they had him, eager to get attention from the students who would be training them for the semester. Slinging his backpack over his shoulder, Connor locked his truck and headed to the barn.

Dust and spiderwebs hung from the rafters, showing the barn's age, but the wood, the concrete, and the foundation were still sound and sturdy. Sunlight came in through windows located in the eaves, causing the spiderwebs to glisten. Hanging on the concrete walls in the entryway were the nameplates of the four breeding stallions who were at the farm. Connor stopped to admire the pictures that hung next to each nameplate. He could see how the weanlings got their good looks. In the pictures, the stallions were racing and jumping, chasing cows, doing what they loved. One showed a large chestnut with a white blaze down his face, clearing a huge jump with ease. Connor was reminded of the large colt he had befriended out in the pasture and guessed that this was his sire. He looked at the nameplate next to the picture: Chromeo. Laughing to himself at the clever name, he examined the other stallions on the wall. Along with Chromeo, there was Disco Fever, Lucky Star, and Stellar. They were each a different breed, a different type, but equally accomplished, and champions in their chosen disciplines. Connor moved closer to read more about each one, but a group of girls came giggling into the barn, interrupting his thoughts. With one last glance at the pictures of the stallions, he followed the girls down the aisle to go to class.

The classroom was small and already filled with students. A large window in the back let in the warm sunlight, accenting the light-yellow paint on the walls. The classroom opened up into the tack room, showing Connor leather bridles and reins hanging on one wall, with saddle racks on the other. Through the tack room, there was a courtyard surrounded by rose bushes. The door was open, letting in the breeze and the sweet chirps of birds.

Greeting each student as they walked in the classroom, a sheet of name tags sat on a stool. The girls ahead of him found their names with ease, their giggling conversation never letting up, and went to find seats. Connor looked but realized there was no name tag for him. He bent down and searched on the ground for a missing sheet but didn't see one.

The instructor for the class, Dr. Carnes, took a few steps in his direction when he noticed Connor looking around. "You must be Connor?"

"Yes, sir." Connor stood up. "I was just trying to find my name tag."

"Well, you don't have one. I don't get many guys in my classes, and you're the only guy among nineteen girls in this one. I already know your name, and I'm sure everyone else will in no time." Dr. Carnes chuckled as he extended his hand out to Connor.

Connor looked around and noticed that he was the

only guy in the room, besides Dr. Carnes. A few of the girls who were listening to their conversation laughed, as Connor did too. "Fair enough." He shook the instructor's hand.

"Welcome to class, Connor."

"Thank you." Connor found a seat and pulled out a notebook and a pen from his backpack. As he opened it to the first page and wrote the date at the top, the last student walked into the classroom.

Connor recognized her, even though he hadn't seen her in years. Yes, she was older, but her striking blue eyes with the specks of gold and her wavy blond ponytail gave her away. It would have taken him a lifetime to forget Caroline Davis. He had watched her at competitions for three years, and she had won every single time. When she rode, she was part of the horse. The two danced together in perfect harmony. No one could tell they were two separate beings; they moved as one. She had shone with confidence and purpose. It was an image that was forever engraved into his brain.

He remembered reading about the accident, the one that had cost her everything. Caroline had been so successful at such a young age. No one ever doubted what she would do with her life or the level of riding she would accomplish. But that had all changed.

Connor knew she had quit riding, and from what he had heard, she didn't interact with horses at all, even though her parents owned and operated one of the most highly regarded training facilities in town. His parents had done business with them for years, selling them horses and breeding ones they already had. Before the accident, Caroline had been following in her mother's footsteps as a professional three-day eventer and had already started helping her by riding and showing their clients' horses.

Scurrying to an empty seat in the same row as Connor, Caroline stuck her name tag to her shirt and sat down. She kept her eyes down as she pulled out a notebook and a pen, the same thing he had just done himself, but there was one difference. Her hands were trembling.

"Alright, everybody, welcome to ANS 271. I'm Dr. Joseph Carnes, and I am your instructor for this class. Let's start by going over the syllabus and filling out some introduction cards. I'll need your emergency contact information, prior horse experience, that kind of stuff." Dr. Carnes began passing out the cards, diverting Connor's attention away from Caroline.

Connor started writing down his information, describing the experience he had gained from nineteen years, his entire life, around horses. He stole glimpses of Caroline as he wrote, watching her close her eyes and clench her fists closed.

God, what is she doing here? She seems so scared, and who could blame her? Connor prayed. *Why is she doing this to herself?*

As he asked those questions, a verse came to mind. Romans 8:28. "And we know that in all things God works for the good of those who love Him, who have been called according to his purpose." Even through his questioning, Connor had to trust that God had a plan. Caroline scooted her chair across the floor, keeping her eyes down at her shoes as the squawk filled the room. She took her card to the front to Dr. Carnes, shocking Connor with how fast she had finished it. He didn't know how she could have written all of her experience down in so little time. She should have had as much as he did, if not more.

Connor took a few more minutes to complete his card

before turning it in. As he sat back down, he looked over at her once more, studying the tension she held in her shoulders and back. Caroline looked up then and caught him watching her. Their eyes met and held. Connor could tell she didn't recognize him, and by the pain, fear, and sadness trapped in her eyes, he thought that might be for the best.

He opened his mouth to say something, to introduce himself, but before he could get any words out, Dr. Carnes spoke, causing both Caroline and Connor to flinch. "I think everyone has handed in their cards, so let's look over the syllabus, and maybe begin our first lecture, if we have time," he announced.

Connor read over the syllabus with the rest of his class and took notes as the lecture began. Dr. Carnes reviewed the birthdates and pedigrees of the weanlings they would be working with over the semester. Connor wrote everything down, smiling to himself when he learned that the bossy chestnut colt from the field, named Rebel, was a son of Chromeo.

Dr. Carnes finished providing the details of the last baby and checked his watch. "I think this is a good place to stop for today. You all can leave your backpacks in here and head out to the pasture for lab. I'll be out in just a few minutes to announce partners and horse assignments."

The class began shuffling around as they put their notebooks into their bags and headed outside, eager to meet their weanlings for the semester. To Connor's surprise, Caroline was one of the first out of the door, darting down the aisle and out of sight. He took his time putting his notebook away, consumed with thoughts about what could have brought her to this class after all she had been through.

He joined his classmates outside as they lined the fence of the weanling pasture. The girls were all chattering away as they admired the babies who were crowding the fence, enjoying the attention. Rebel was pushing his way through his playmates, just as he had been earlier. Connor searched for that wavy blond ponytail, but he didn't see Caroline anywhere.

Turning around, he glanced back at the barn. He saw her standing alone in the aisle, studying the pictures of the stallions, as he had done before the lecture. Without hesitation, he left the group and went to her.

He paused in the doorway, watching her as she looked at the pictures and nameplates. She reached out and brushed the picture of Stellar with her fingers, her hand still shaking.

"He's something to look at, isn't he?" Connor took a couple of steps closer to her. Caroline gasped and whirled around, startled by Connor's voice. "I'm sorry. I didn't mean to scare you."

Caroline gulped. "It's okay. I didn't know anyone was still in here. I thought everyone was outside."

Their eyes held again, like they had in the classroom. Connor studied the worry in her eyes and debated about telling her he knew who she was. As Caroline looked away, he decided to keep his secret to himself.

"Do you know about his racing career?" He pointed toward the plaque on the wall.

Caroline's eyes turned back to the picture of Stellar. The almost-black stallion was photographed in a full gallop, from his prime as a racehorse. "Yeah." She crossed her arms as she answered, almost under her breath. "He won everything he ever ran in, except for the last one, when he injured his suspensory ligament."

Connor smiled at her. "Bred for a couple years in Kentucky, then came out here," he added. Caroline nodded her head, not taking her eyes off the picture. "I'm Connor Taylor."

She looked up at him then. "Caroline Davis." She gave him a small, tentative smile.

"Nice to meet you. Have you had a chance to look at the weanlings yet?"

Caroline looked down at her boots. "Um, no. No, I haven't," she said.

"They're all pretty special, and we should probably head out there now." Connor glanced toward the field. "Come on, I'll show you."

He could sense her hesitation, but she followed him anyway. They walked side by side in silence to the fence. "Do you see that big chestnut colt over there?" He pointed across the pasture. "That's Rebel. He seems to be in charge. He pushes his way through the herd to do whatever he wants."

Caroline stared out at the field, watching Rebel interact with the other babies. "You're right. You must have spent some time studying them."

"Just a few minutes before class. He's so bossy, it was easy to pick up on."

Caroline nodded, not taking her eyes off the young horses. Connor looked down and noticed her hands were still shaking.

"Alright, everybody, listen up," Dr. Carnes announced as he came out of the barn. "I've made the horse and partner assignments based off the experience you wrote down on your intro cards. I've paired students with experience up with those who have little experience, and tried to match horse personalities accordingly, as well.

Of course, it isn't a perfect science, so there may be some adjustments during these first few weeks." Dr. Carnes looked down at his clipboard and began reading off names and horse assignments.

"Do you have an idea which one you want?" Connor lowered his voice, so they wouldn't interrupt their instructor. He watched her swallow before she answered.

"No, not really." She bit her lip. "What about you?"

"Nah, I don't have a preference. I'm just excited to take this class, ya know?"

Caroline stared at him, and once again Connor could read the anxiety in her expression. She opened her mouth to say something but closed it before the words ever left.

"Caroline Davis?" Dr. Carnes searched the group of students. Caroline lifted and turned her head in response. "Your partner is Connor, and you guys will be working with Luna, the dark bay thoroughbred filly with the crescent moon–shaped marking on her head."

Adrenaline rushed through Connor's body as he realized he would get to work with Caroline for the next several weeks. Together they turned to the field to look for their horse. She was in the middle of the herd, encircled by her playmates.

"Looks like we've got the social butterfly of the group." As Connor spoke, Rebel pushed his way through the horses, bumping into Luna's shoulder as he went. Luna pinned her ears and bit Rebel on the rump, causing him to squeal and run off.

"Or not." Caroline glanced at Connor with eyes of doubt.

Connor laughed. "Somebody has to put Rebel in his place."

"Alright, I think that's everybody," Dr. Carnes interrupted. "For lab today, we are just going to go in and meet your babies."

Connor heard Caroline suck in a quick breath. "Are you okay?" Connor questioned as they followed their classmates and teacher to the gate.

"Yeah." She avoided making eye contact. Connor studied her, and by her pale face and worried eyes, he knew that she wasn't.

"It'll be alright. They all seem pretty friendly." Connor tried to reassure her, but Caroline only nodded.

The chain around the gate rattled as Dr. Carnes undid the clip on the end. He pushed the gate in, against the grass in the pasture. The young horses crowded around to greet all of the students. Connor made sure to keep Caroline close by. Dr. Carnes pointed out which baby was which. After just a few minutes, each pair had found their weanling.

Connor approached Luna first, as Caroline stayed next to the fence, away from the horses. He held his hand out to her as he got closer, and the filly stretched her neck until her nose touched him. As Luna breathed in his scent, Connor took one more step to her and scratched her on the shoulder.

He glanced back at Caroline. "She's a sweetheart. You can come a little closer."

"I'm okay here."

Connor continued to scratch Luna. "I really think it'll be okay. Come get to know her."

With small steps, Caroline drug herself away from the fence line and walked to Connor and Luna. The little horse flicked her ears forward, watching Caroline. As she got closer, she whinnied at her.

"See, she likes you already." Connor grinned at her.

Caroline looked at him, pausing after every small step she took, but she kept coming.

Caroline lifted her shaking hand out for Luna to see. The weanling took a step forward and pressed her muzzle into Caroline's palm, licking her with her soft pink tongue. Connor watched as her shoulders relaxed, and a soft smile came across her face.

"I told you." Connor continued petting the horse's shoulder.

"Yeah, I guess you did." Caroline rubbed Luna on her black forehead, right where the white crescent moon sat. "She's pretty."

"Yeah, she is." He took a step back to look at their horse. "And she's built well too. She looks a lot like Stellar."

Caroline snapped her eyes up to his. "Why do you say that?"

"She's the only foal by him this year, if I'm remembering Dr. Carnes' lecture correctly."

"Oh, right," Caroline mumbled as the smile faded from her lips. She kept petting Luna, but Connor could sense something was bothering her again.

"Okay, everybody. That's all for today. We'll continue with lecture on Wednesday, and for lab we will start working on teaching these guys how to walk on a lead." Dr. Carnes began walking toward the gate.

"Bye, Luna. See you Wednesday," Connor gave her one last pat before they turned to follow their instructor out of the field. They walked without speaking until they were in the classroom.

"Do you have any other classes today?" He broke the silence as he and Caroline grabbed their bags.

"Yeah, chemistry, unfortunately."

"Ugh, good luck with that. It's not easy."

"I was afraid of that." Caroline checked her watch. "I better get going. I'll see you Wednesday."

"Sounds good," Connor gave her a small wave.

Caroline walked out of the classroom as Connor finished gathering up his stuff. Most of the other girls had already walked out when Dr. Carnes walked in.

"Oh good, Connor, you're still here. I wanted to talk to you for a minute."

"Yes, sir?"

"You have the most horse experience in the class, which is why I put you with Caroline. She doesn't have any, and she seems anxious. Luna is sweet, but if she's anything like her mother, or her siblings, there's a stubborn and ornery streak in there that will show up from time to time. So just keep an eye out for that, and make sure to help Caroline through it, and feel free to take over with something if you think you need to."

Connor raised his eyebrows in confusion. "I'm sorry, sir, you said Caroline doesn't have any horse experience?"

"That's right. But I think you'll be able to help her catch up to the others. Are you okay with that?"

"Yes, yes, I am." Connor nodded his head, blinking to hide his surprise.

"Good. Have a good day, Connor."

"Thank you. You too."

Connor walked to his truck, trying to make sense of what he just learned. Why would Caroline take the class if she was so scared? Why would she lie about her experience? He didn't have the answers to his questions, but he knew someone who did.

God, You know why. Can You show me the answers? Can You help me see what I am supposed to do?

As he prayed, the verse from earlier came back to his

mind. God had a purpose, a good purpose. He would just have to wait and see what happened, what plan God had in mind for the class, and for Caroline. And what reason she had for lying.

In the meantime, he would do whatever he could do to help her.

Three

BY THE FOURTH STOPLIGHT on the way to the main campus, Caroline's hands stopped shaking and she managed to take her first full breath in two hours. She wasn't sure she could last a whole semester of feeling like this, but she wasn't sure what other option she had. She needed a major, and horses had once meant everything to her. And maybe they could again.

Turning into her parking garage, Caroline's eyes locked onto the giant red, blue, and white block A on the athletic building across the street. She stared at it as she waited for the electric arm of the parking barrier to lift and let her in. She found a spot on the second floor. Glancing at herself in the rearview mirror, she was shocked to see how pale and clammy her face was. Her bangs were curling in response to the dampness of her forehead. All she wanted to do was go home, but chemistry and her first softball practice as a manager stood in her way. She tore herself away from her reflection and forced herself to get out of the car.

As she walked out of the garage, Caroline pulled her phone out of the front zipper pocket of her backpack to check her schedule for the building and room number for her class. She saw she had missed three texts from Ryan while she had been at the farm and driving.

12:45 PM: Hey babe, still meeting
before practice?

1:23 PM: Hello? You there?

1:42 PM: Least you could do is
acknowledge me.

Caroline sighed. Ryan was not the most patient person, something she had learned in the three years they had been together. He liked making plans and sticking to them and got frustrated when they changed or fell through at the last minute. He was the star shortstop for the baseball team and was focused on playing professional baseball. She texted back.

2:40 PM: Hey, sorry, I was in class,
then driving. Yes, I'll meet you in the
union after chem.

She opened the university app, found the information for her class, and began walking. Ryan answered her just a moment later.

2:41 PM: Great!

Well that was an easy fix, she thought to herself. *If only everything could be that simple.* All around her students hustled by, chatting and laughing as they headed to their classes. Their excitement was easy to feel, but she couldn't share in it. She just wanted the day to be over.

She located the building and room for her class and took a seat near the back, the cold metal of the chair pressing into her back. She pulled out her notebook and began to flip past the notes she had taken in weanling class. She paused, studying the shaky chicken scratch that filled the pages. She couldn't decipher her own handwriting.

She flipped over to a clean page. At least her hand would be steady for this lecture. Scribbled handwriting wouldn't be the reason she couldn't understand her notes for this class. Science was her least favorite subject, and chemistry wouldn't be easy for her.

Caroline tried to follow along with her professor, but her mind kept drifting to Ryan. They had met their sophomore year of high school, when they had both made varsity, he in baseball, and she in softball. Focused on their sports, they had found common ground in wanting to be the best. They ran together and lifted weights, went to the batting cages and played catch, challenging each other to continue to improve and cheering each other on as they did. When they both received scholarship offers to the same school, they thought they'd be together forever.

But in the last few weeks, Caroline hadn't been so sure. Ryan had been great since her injury and was doing his best to support her, but he couldn't relate to how it had affected her. Sometimes, it was hard for her to be around him, listening to him talk about baseball and his dreams. It wasn't his fault he could still play, and she couldn't, but that fact didn't make it any easier for her to accept.

Caroline blinked herself free from her thoughts and managed to take a few focused notes on the organization of the periodic table before the class ended. She packed up her things, imagining the reading and Googling she would have to do on her own time to understand the lecture she had just daydreamed through. Day one and she was already falling behind.

She ambled toward the student union, eyeing the sprinklers as they sprayed down the grass on the mall, filling her nose with the false hope of rain. The sun danced on the water droplets as they were suspended in the air, giving them a shiny exterior before they plummeted to the ground. The drops had no control over where they landed. That's how Caroline was feeling about her life.

She turned around one last corner and saw Ryan in their usual meeting spot, leaning against a pillar, one leg bent at the knee with his foot pushing against it. His blond hair was hidden under his navy baseball cap, and the sturdy muscles in his forearms moved as he scrolled through whatever he was looking at on his phone. He was so intent on the screen that he didn't see her until she walked right up to him. His sea-green eyes lifted to hers, and even after years of being together, his smile still brought heat to her cheeks.

"There you are." Ryan pushed off the pillar and kissed her cheek. Caroline searched his face and took note of the extra sparkle in his expression.

"Hey, what's going on?" Caroline closed her fingers around his as he took her hand and led her into the union. "You seem extra happy."

"You noticed." He beamed at her. "Well, I am. The fall ball preseason polls came out today, and they have us ranked as number one in the conference. My name is also being circulated around by some MLB scouts, so it's been a pretty good day."

Caroline tried to force a smile as her heart dropped in her chest. She was thrilled for him, but at the same time, his success was another reminder of everything she had lost. "That's great." She squeezed his hand.

"Isn't it?" He was still beaming, not picking up on her sadness. "You hungry? The usual?"

"Yeah, sounds good." Ryan led her into the line for Chick-Fil-A and continued talking about his day.

"I love my schedule this semester. Taking these online

classes was a great decision. It's freed up so much time during the day. I can hit in the cage or weight lift basically whenever I want. It'll really help me get my power hitting numbers up from the left. I need to get them equal with my numbers from the right side, ya know? Keep those scouts talking." Ryan finished his thought without taking a breath. He stepped up to the counter and ordered their food. After he paid and took the bag, he went right back to talking about his plans. Caroline tuned him out as she grabbed napkins and ketchup, then followed him to an open table.

They slid into the booth and Ryan handed her one of the chicken sandwiches from the bag. "I just feel like this is my year, ya know? To make some noise and get drafted, start making things happen." He paused to take a bite.

Caroline nodded her head as she chewed. Between each bite, Ryan kept on talking. It was easy for her to see how excited he was about all of this, as he should be. He had worked hard, and it was starting to pay off for him. She just wished that she could share in his success, or at least feel the same joy he was experiencing.

"Caroline? Did you hear me?"

"Yeah. That's all really great, Ry. I'm happy for you."

"Just gotta keep working." He smiled. "What about you? You excited for practice?"

She stopped chewing. "Why would you ask that?"

Ryan paused, swallowing and blinking before he answered her. "I just meant if you were excited to see everyone and help out. I think it's awesome you still get to be a part of the team."

"Even if it is 'awesome,' it's not the same. I think it's going to be really hard for me." She looked down at the table.

Ryan hesitated once again, unsure of what to say. He cleared his throat, buying time. "Well, how were your classes? What did you have today?"

She lifted her eyes to his and saw that he was asking this question with sincerity. He didn't remember what she had had to do today. "I had stats and chem, and my first class at the farm," she muttered.

"How'd that go?"

"It was okay. I'm not sure I can handle it, though."

"Then why do it? You could probably find something else if you're worried about credit hours." Ryan dipped a waffle fry down into the ketchup.

"I'm not worried about credits, but—"

"Then just drop it. Find something else to do," Ryan interrupted. "Seems simple enough to me."

Caroline stared at him. "It's not that simple. I need a major, Ryan. What else am I supposed to do?"

"Honey, haven't you been listening? Scouts are talking about me. My ticket to the big leagues is pretty much punched. You don't need anything else but me. Our futures are set. Who cares about school?"

She searched his eyes and his face to see if he was kidding in a misguided attempt to make her feel better. Sure enough, there was a goofy grin and a twinkle of silliness in his expression. Caroline crumbled up her sandwich wrapper, half of her sandwich uneaten, and threw it in the empty bag. "I have to get going." She stood up, her chair squealing on the tile floor.

"Caroline, I was just kidding. What did I do?" Ryan's shock echoed in every word.

"Nothing. You're fine. I just need to go. I'll talk to you later." Caroline threw her backpack over her shoulder and walked away from the table without a look behind her.

Four

CAROLINE KEPT HER HEAD DOWN as she walked, her mind swirling from being at the farm, her time with Ryan, and the idea of seeing her teammates and being on the field again. The field used to be her escape, her refuge, but now, she was dreading it.

A quick glimpse around the batting cages and the dugout showed her she was alone, the first to arrive for practice. The back gate squeaked as she pushed it open and entered the bullpen, the place where she had spent so many hours working on spins and velocity. She shuffled over to the off-white pitching rubber and stared down to home plate. She ran her thumb over the third finger on her right hand and pretended her callous was still there, molded from the seam of the ball burning her skin as it spun away toward the batter.

A blue crate of softballs sat to her left. Caroline turned toward it, thinking about the weight of the ball in her hand. She reached out, feeling the seams with just the tips of her fingers. It was the first time she had touched one since her last game, and it still felt like home.

Without giving it a second thought, she picked up the ball, dropped her backpack to the red clay dirt, and went back to the pitching rubber. She lined up her feet, placing each one with more purpose and exactness than she ever had before. She rolled the ball around in her hand, thinking about the possibility, the chance, that the doctors were wrong.

Just one pitch. One throw, and I can prove them all wrong, she thought to herself. *One strike, that's all I need. Then I can feel the excitement and joy Ryan has. Then I can have a purpose again.* Caroline shifted her weight to her left foot, imagining the signal from her catcher. She rocked back, picturing where she wanted the ball to go. She took her stride toward the batter, wound her right arm up and around, and released, snapping the ball off next to her hip. The ball slammed to the ground right in front of her and skidded its way to home plate. Pain shot through her forearm and elbow, taking her breath away. She gripped her arm and went down to her knees, gasping for air. She didn't stay down for long, in fear that someone would discover her. She shoved herself up and off the ground. With angry tears in her eyes, she retrieved the ball and banged it back into the cart. She grabbed her bag and stomped her way down the steps and into the dugout.

She sat down on the bench, the rough wood poking her through her shorts. She rubbed away the pain in her arm, until it turned to tingling. She opened and closed her fist, working to get feeling back. Two tears trickled down from her eyes. As she wiped them away with the back of her left hand, she heard someone clear his throat. She turned toward the entrance to the dugout and saw her coach, Ben Sullivan.

Caroline sat up and blinked any remaining tears away as Coach Sullivan came and sat near her on the bench. He didn't say anything for a moment, and just sat there staring out at the field. Caroline waited, pulling at a string on her shirt.

"How badly did you just hurt yourself?" He gave her a

sideways glance.

"You saw." Caroline sighed.

"Yeah, I did. You okay?"

Caroline wiggled her fingers. "Yeah, I am."

Coach Sullivan studied her with kind brown eyes. "Did I ever tell you why I never played baseball beyond college?"

"No, you didn't."

"It's not a long story. It comes down to the fact that I'm shorter than your average athlete, you could use an hourglass to time me running the bases, and no major league team wanted me. Simple stuff." He shrugged his shoulders, a slight grin on his face.

"Coach..."

"Hang on, let me finish." He looked over at her, kindness in his eyes. "I was devastated, angry at God, didn't think it was fair at all. The life I had planned for myself no longer made sense. But you know what?"

"What?" Caroline crossed her arms.

"The sun came up the next day. And the next. And the next. Life went on. Eventually, I had to decide to, too. It didn't come easily, and it didn't come immediately. All I'm trying to say is one day, something will make sense again. God has a better plan than any of us ever could."

"I'm not so sure," she muttered.

"That's okay, you don't have to be sure right now." Coach Sullivan slapped the bench and stood up. "Looks like the other girls are showing up. Come shag for me for the fielding drills."

"Yes, sir." Caroline made herself stand as the girls came flooding into the dugout. They all started squealing her name and hugging her as they came in. She faked a smile through it all.

Caroline started to climb up the steps from the dugout

and on to the field, but the pitching coach, Tara Morris, stopped her.

"Caroline, can you come here a second?" Tara called from the bullpen.

Caroline looked up and saw the pitchers and catchers setting up for their drills. Coach Tara was waving her toward them. She sighed and headed that way.

"Caroline, it's good to see you." Her coach gave her a hug. "How are you doing?"

"Good." Caroline smiled to cover her fib.

"Good." Coach Tara smiled back. "There's someone I want you to meet. Our freshman pitcher. Sarah?"

A tall brunette with a long, curly ponytail turned and looked up from her bat bag. A huge smile lit up her hazel eyes as she hurried toward Caroline.

"Sarah Hansen, this is—" Coach Tara started.

"Caroline Davis." Sarah interrupted. "Oh my gosh, I can't believe I'm meeting you!" The girl squealed as she shook Caroline's hand.

Caroline tried to hide her shock at the sudden outburst. "Nice to meet you too, Sarah," she mumbled.

"I am such a fan. I've watched every single game you threw last year, probably twice. I have them all recorded. I just really admire you, and I can't believe I'm here meeting you!" Sarah paused to take a short breath, and a more serious look crossed her face. "I'm so sorry about your arm though. I can't even imagine what it must be like."

Caroline saw pity in the freshman's eyes and spoke up to turn the conversation away from her. "That's alright." Caroline took a step away from Sarah. "Things happen. It just means you have some pretty big shoes to fill, right?"

Sarah's excitement returned. "Yes, yes, I do. And I'm ready to work as hard as ever."

"Alright, Sarah, go ahead and get warmed up and we'll start today's workout." Coach Tara pointed toward a target that had been set up.

"Yes ma'am!" She turned back to her bag and pulled out her glove and her shoes. Caroline bit her lip to hide the emotions she was fighting.

"Caroline, I'm sorry." Coach Tara touched her on the arm. "I didn't know she'd go there."

"It's fine." Caroline jerked her arm away. "I need to go shag for Coach Sullivan."

"Alright, well if you finish with that, I'd love your help over here."

"We'll see." She walked away and headed back toward the field.

If there was one thing Caroline hated in life, it was being pitied. She had dealt with it before, and here she was again. She walked to home plate, where a glove was waiting for her next to the coach's bat and the buckets of balls. She pushed her left hand into the leather and paused as she felt the old rush of adrenaline. She pulled the glove to her nose, closed her eyes, and inhaled the sweet, salty scent.

Maybe it was the pity she had seen in Sarah's eyes, or the class she had endured at the farm earlier that day, but the smell of the leather glove didn't remind her of the game or of her time on the mound. The scent brought back a different memory from an earlier life, a life that had ended five years ago.

Fourteen-year-old Caroline's phone chirped on the nightstand next to her, interrupting her reading of the magazine she held in her hand. She flipped the cover shut and reached for it, cringing as her ribs reminded her not to move without thinking it through. It had been two months since the wreck, but her injuries were still healing.

> Mom, 10:03 AM: Hey honey, feel up
> to coming down to the barn for a
> little bit?

Her breath caught in her throat as she read the message. She hadn't been to the barn since she'd come home from the hospital earlier that week. The place where she used to spend more time than anywhere else had become the place she avoided.

Caroline looked out of her bedroom window toward the barn. The September sun was glinting off the roof, holding on to the last heatwave of the Arizona desert's summer. Despite the high temperatures, the parking area was full, with the usual Saturday morning busyness. A handful of people were on their horses heading out for a trail ride on the cross-country course in the back fields. Her mom was always swamped with lessons on the weekends, but she must have had a short break if she was asking Caroline to come down. She turned her attention back to the text message and sighed as she responded.

> 10:05 AM: Sure, be right there

She stood up from her bed, being careful not to hurt her ribs again or jostle her left wrist, which was still in a cast. She made it down the stairs one step at a time and managed to pull on her boots with one hand. She reached for the doorknob, fingering the cold metal, questioning if she had the emotional strength to go outside as her phone chirped again from her pocket.

> Mom, 10:09 AM :)

The simple smiley from her mom was enough encouragement for her to open the door and step outside. She kept her eyes down on the ground as she shuffled her way to the barn, trying to go unseen so she wouldn't have to talk to anyone. She was tired of being asked how she was, or worse, being told how sorry they were for her.

Caroline walked through the back entrance of the barn and paused. Her eyes needed a few seconds to adjust to the dim, dusty light. A few horses were chewing their hay as they looked out their stall doors at her. She walked past them, her gaze locking on the nameplate, *Beaus and Ribbons,* that was still hanging by the empty stall five doors down.

The stall door was open, and she couldn't help but stop in its threshold. Without much thought, her hand reached up and touched the wooden name. The stall had been stripped since he had been there, and fresh shavings covered the mats. His empty black water buckets hung by the empty hay net, mirroring how she felt.

Her parents' voices coming from the office tore her away from the stall. She followed the sound and found them on the computer.

"Oh, Caroline, there you are. Come on in." Holly Davis greeted her. "We found a couple of horses we want to show you."

Caroline slinked into the office and felt the blood draining from her face. Her dad stood and offered her his chair. She lowered herself into it without moving her upper body. Her dad put his hand on her good arm to steady her.

"There are dozens out there right now." Her mom grinned and pointed at the screen. "But we thought we'd start with these three, if you like them as much as we do."

Caroline nodded and went through the motions of studying each horse. Her mom talked her through the ads for two mares and a gelding, all three of them with experience at the highest level of eventing. They were all remarkable, and all beautiful, but all she could picture was Beau, and that final jump. Her heart rate kept climbing and the back of her neck grew cold with sweat as she remembered.

"What do you think, sweetie?" Her dad squeezed her shoulder. "Wanna go see a couple of these guys?"

Panic rose to her throat and forced her to gasp for air. Tears spilled over her face. "I can't. I'm sorry, I just can't." She got up and fled from the office, her ribs and wrist burning as she went.

"Caroline, wait..." she heard her parents calling after her, but she didn't stop. She was heading for the back entrance but saw a couple of people standing in the aisle. She ducked into the tack room and ended up in the back corner, where no one could see or hear her.

She worked to get air into her lungs and her tears dried up. The pain from her quick movements dissolved with every breath. She stood there, looking at the bridles hanging in front of her. The sweet leather scent filled her nose, calling to her to touch the reins dangling within reach. Her fingers closed around them, muscle memory taking over as her wrists turned so her thumbs sat on top of her hands. Proper position would be engrained in her mind forever.

"I can't believe it. Do you really think it's true?" A hushed voice came from the front part of the tack room. Caroline recognized Abby's voice, one of her closest friends.

"I do." Another girl, Katy, responded. "Think about it.

She's been home for a week, and no one has seen her."

"That doesn't mean she's quitting." Abby placed her saddle on the rack. "If you had been through what she has been through, don't you think you'd avoid this place for a while too?"

"Maybe. But not if I was as talented as her. Accidents happen, it's part of the sport. Then you gotta move past it." Katy crossed her arms over her chest.

"I guess you're right." Abby shrugged, defeated. "It's a shame though. I feel so bad for her. It's like she's lost everything."

Caroline couldn't hear Katy's response as their footsteps down the barn aisle drowned out their voices. She waited a few minutes to make sure they were gone before she snuck out of the barn and back to the house.

Back in her room, she stared at the pictures, the ribbons, and the trophies that surrounded her on the walls and shelves in her room. Even her closest friends pitied her and were talking about her. But Katy had been right. It was time to move past it.

She found a couple of boxes in the hall closet and went to work, taking down every picture, every ribbon, and every trophy, shoving them to the back of her closet where she wouldn't have to look at them.

Lifting her nose from the glove, Caroline blinked to clear her thoughts. She hadn't wanted to be pitied. She hadn't wanted people talking about her. She had been determined to find success again. She had chosen horses over softball, which had been the wrong choice. Maybe the accident had given her a chance to start over, to make the right choice, to follow her dad's path. She had made plans to become the greatest softball pitcher she could be, so no one would ever feel bad for her or pity her again. But she was right back where she had started.

"Caroline, are you ready?" Coach Sullivan picked up the bat and a ball.

"Yep." She lifted her lips up into a small smile.

"Let's get at it, then."

They got into a rhythm as the fielding drills began, with him hitting the balls to the girls on the field, and her catching the throws that came back in to home plate. The ting of the bat and the pop of her glove became a song in her head, causing her to tune out the struggles of her day, causing her to forget how much had changed in the last couple of months. It was a simple exercise, catching and tossing the ball, but it was what she needed.

"Alright, everyone, that was great," Coach Sullivan called out, ending practice long before she was ready to quit and return to reality. "Let's rake and clean up and call it a day."

Caroline helped the girls put everything away and turned down several offers to hang out or do homework with the team. She recognized the looks they were giving her, as they were the same ones Abby and Katy, and a dozen others, had given her five years ago, after the accident. She walked to her car and drove home in silence, wishing she wasn't in a position to be pitied again. She had dealt with it the last time. She had overcome their feelings by focusing on pitching. But this was different. This time, she knew she wouldn't be able to find something else to be great at. This time, she didn't have any options.

Five

THE GOLDEN BUCKLE OF THE SOFT PINK HALTER glinted in the sun and rattled in Caroline's hand as Connor saw her walking toward the pasture. They had just finished their second lecture, and it was time to begin halter breaking their babies. He had watched her take notes again, and though her shaking was still there, she had seemed a little more in control.

At least in the lecture.

Her anxious blue eyes looked up at him as she stopped near the gate. Her hands worked the straps of the halter, wringing them through her fingers, as she bit her lip. "Um...do you wanna go first?"

"Sure thing." Connor took the halter from her. "You got the lead rope?"

"Yep, got it."

They stood by the gate while the rest of their class got their halters and ropes. Caroline dug her toe in the dirt, drawing small circles with her boot as they waited.

"Have you ever done this before?" Caroline asked as she continued her scuffling.

"Yeah, quite a bit actually."

"Really?"

"Yeah. My parents run a pretty large breeding farm. I've been helping out as long as I can remember."

Caroline stopped playing in the dirt and looked up at

him. "Here in Tucson?"

"No, about sixty miles southeast of here."

"Sonoita?"

"Yep, that's the place."

Caroline blinked and tilted her head as Dr. Carnes came out of the barn and began opening the gate. "Remember guys, if you don't get your halter on today, that's okay. We are just aiming to get them used to it around their head and face. Anything beyond that is just icing on the cake. I'd rather you go slow than skip the little steps. I'll be making the rounds and helping out wherever I'm needed."

"Ready?" Connor slowed his steps to match Caroline's as they began trudging through the knee-high grass of the pasture.

"Yeah." She exhaled as she whipped her hair up into a ponytail. "Let's get started."

Connor approached Luna with the halter in his right hand at his side, keeping it low and out of the horse's vision. She looked up at him with curious eyes and took a few steps toward him.

"Hi, good girl. We're gonna try something new today, how does that sound?" He spoke with a gentle voice as he reached out and rubbed the filly on her shoulder with his knuckles.

Luna turned her head toward him and nibbled at the sleeve of his shirt, grabbing it with her small teeth. "Nice try, little missy," Connor corrected, pushing her nose away with just one finger, disciplining the young horse without being too harsh.

"Are you okay?" Caroline stuttered from a few feet behind him.

"Yep, she wasn't being mean. Just being a playful baby." Connor answered in the same voice he was using on Luna.

"She just got my shirt."

Connor fought the urge to turn around and look at Caroline. He wanted to check on her but knew he couldn't take his focus off Luna. He kept scratching the horse's shoulder as he took slow, careful movements to put the halter in his other hand.

The young horse stiffened her muscles as she felt the neoprene straps touch her skin. Her ears shifted back, communicating to Connor that she was unsure about what was happening. He heard Caroline's breath catch in her throat.

"Hey, it's alright. No one is going to hurt you. This is all a part of the plan. Everything is going to be just fine." Connor wasn't sure if he was speaking more to Luna, or to Caroline.

He continued rubbing Luna with the halter, and as the tension in her muscles eased, her ears started to relax. She dropped her head a couple of inches and licked her lips, a sign of acceptance. "See, Caroline? She's already starting to relax."

Caroline didn't answer him, and again he struggled with wanting to check on her. *God, help her relax,* he prayed. He just kept doing what he was doing, working the halter up toward the filly's head, moving just a few finger breadths at a time. Luna didn't tense up or resist again, and when Connor got the halter up near her nose, she tried to take it in her teeth, like she had with his shirt sleeve earlier.

"Alright, little one, let's give you a break." Connor laughed as he lowered the halter from her nose. He gave her a pat on the neck, then turned to Caroline.

She was standing with her arms wrapped around her middle, like she was holding herself together. Her face was pasty, her eyes were concerned, but a small, tense smile was stretched over her lips.

"You're good at this." Her words were just loud enough for him to hear.

"Nah, just lots of practice. And she definitely isn't scared of this thing." He gestured toward the halter. "Just had to test her boundaries, I think."

"Well, still. You did everything you were supposed to."

"She makes it pretty easy." Connor rubbed the moon-shaped marking on Luna's forehead. "Wanna come say hi to her?"

He watched Caroline hesitate before she nodded her head and took a few steps toward them. Luna looked up and gave a soft nicker as she approached.

"She knows you already. Or she just wants you to rescue her from me." Connor grinned.

Caroline rolled her eyes as she reached her hand out for Luna to smell. The filly snorted, blowing warm air on Caroline's fingers.

"No nibbling on me, alright? I'm not as tasty as he is." Caroline looked up at Connor through her eyelashes, teasing both the horse and him.

"Hey now, no ganging up on me here, girls."

"Just stating the obvious." Luna sneezed and stomped her foot in agreement.

"I'm the only guy in this class. You'd think I'd at least get to work with a colt." Connor laughed with a shake of his head. "You ready to try the halter?"

"Um...don't you think she's had enough for today? She was pretty good, and like Dr. Carnes said, better to go too slow than to do too much too soon."

"I think she's okay for another go if you wanna try it. She didn't overreact or get upset."

Caroline swallowed and looked from Luna to Connor.

"You'll be right here? If something happens?"

"Of course. I'm not going anywhere. But nothing is gonna happen."

Caroline gave a short nod as she took the halter from Connor and approached Luna's shoulder. As she reached out to touch the filly, she glanced back at Connor.

"It'll be fine. Just start how I did, pet her on the shoulder with your empty hand then gradually incorporate the halter."

Caroline turned back to the horse. She reached out with unsteady fingers toward the filly. Luna watched her with a soft, quiet interest.

Connor studied Caroline's every move, taking note of the skill she showed even through her apprehension. She was patient and stayed with Luna as she tensed up again, giving up the fight even quicker than she had with Connor. As she got the halter to the filly's nose, Luna dropped her head and sighed, accepting what Caroline was asking of her. Dr. Carnes walked up behind them.

"Looks like things are going very well with her. I think she's ready for you to put it on, Caroline. What do you think?" Dr. Carnes stopped a few feet away from where they were working.

Connor saw a flash of panic shoot through Caroline. "Maybe Connor should do it?" Her knuckles whitened on the halter.

"You're okay." Dr. Carnes encouraged her. "Look how quiet she's being with you. I think you've got it. We'll be right here."

Caroline met Connor's gaze, so he smiled at her. "You can do it."

"Alright." She sighed as she looked back at Luna.

"I want you to keep ahold of the noseband with your

left hand and reach over her head with your right. Before you grab the crownpiece, take a few moments to pet her by her ear and that side of her head, so she knows you're there." Dr. Carnes guided her as his eyes swept over the pasture, making sure everyone else was still doing okay.

Caroline did as he said, following each step with care so she wouldn't startle the filly. Again, Connor was impressed by the precision of her actions, even more so than before, since he could see how nervous she still was. She reached her hand over Luna's head and caressed Luna's cheek. The horse lifted her head and the muscles in her neck went rigid, but Caroline continued to pet her.

"It's okay." Caroline breathed. "We're going to be fine."

As she whispered, Luna's left ear rotated toward Caroline, a sign that she was listening to her. Connor watched as Luna's muscles softened. Caroline continued to stroke her, and Luna dropped her head.

"Good, Caroline. When you're ready, reach for the crownpiece and bring it over her head, and into the buckle," Dr. Carnes instructed.

Caroline did as she was told, and Connor watched as Luna didn't react or tense up. She stood still, and as Caroline buckled the halter over her head, she turned to look at Caroline with nothing but light and tranquility in her eyes.

"Great job. I'd leave it on for a few minutes, then take it off. I'm going to check on the other students, but let me know if you need help." Dr. Carnes started to walk away.

"Thank you, sir." Connor moved closer to Caroline and their horse. Caroline stood there staring at Luna, and Connor could see her legs quivering. "You okay?"

Caroline closed her eyes and took a long breath in through her nose. "Yeah." She pushed the air out of her mouth.

"That was awesome to watch. You're a natural." Connor complimented her, petting Luna at the same time.

"No, I'm not. I'm really not."

"Yes, you are. She was totally in tune with you and—"

"Connor," she interrupted, staring at him as she did.

He could see the hurt reflecting in her face. He cleared his throat. "Yeah?"

"I didn't do much. You did the hard stuff."

"No, I didn't. I didn't put the halter on her. That was all you."

"Connor, please." Caroline begged. "Stop. I'm not good at this at all."

"Okay."

"Thank you." She wiped her sweaty palms on her jeans.

"No problem."

Caroline looked down at the grass, blinking several times. Connor heard her sniff, and realized she was trying to keep herself from crying. Before he could say or do anything to comfort her, her shiny eyes snapped back up to his.

"It wasn't me. It was all her." She shrugged toward Luna.

"Yeah, she's a good girl." Connor felt a lump forming in his own throat. He coughed to clear it before she could notice. "Do you think we should take the halter off now?"

"Yeah, she's probably ready. Do you want to do it?"

"Sure thing." Connor reached for Luna's shoulder. He followed the same process as they had to put the halter on. The small horse stood still as Connor unbuckled the strap and lowered it from her face. When the halter was off, Luna shook her head, flopping her ears against the side of her head.

"I guess she's celebrating." Connor laughed, patting the

filly's neck.

"She deserves to. She was a pro."

"Alright, everyone, let's find a good place to stop. That'll be all for today," Dr. Carnes announced from near the gate.

"Good timing." Connor gave Luna one last scratch on her shoulder. "Bye, little girl. We'll see you later."

"See ya, Luna." Caroline reached and lay her fingers on Luna's cheek. Luna stretched her neck out and rested her muzzle on Caroline's shoulder, just for a moment, before turning away to find her friends in the pasture.

"She likes you," Connor mentioned as they began their trek back through the grass.

"She just likes attention," Caroline told him.

"Maybe," he answered, deciding not to push the issue based on the conversation from earlier.

They walked in silence to the gate and into the classroom to get their bags. As they walked back outside to the parking area, Connor had an idea.

"Hey, Caroline?"

"Yeah?"

"If you're not doing anything this weekend, maybe you'd like to come down to my parents' farm? It's a few degrees cooler down there, so it might be a good chance to get out of this heat." Connor shrugged his shoulders.

He watched the range of emotions spread out across her face before fear and sadness settled in. "Um, this weekend probably won't work. I'm pretty busy, between softball practice and homework, that kind of stuff."

"You play softball?"

"Um, no, I'm just the manager. But I still have to go to practice."

"I gotcha. Well, maybe some other time, then. I go home most weekends to help out, so just let me know if you ever want to come." Connor opened the door to his truck.

"Yeah, I'll let you know."

"Sounds good. Have a good afternoon, Caroline."

"You too." She turned and walked away. Connor climbed into the driver's seat, as she stopped and turned back toward him.

"Connor?"

"Yeah?"

"Thank you."

"You're welcome. Remember, anytime you want, just let me know."

Caroline nodded her head as she continued to her car. Connor shut his door and stared at his steering wheel, Caroline's sad eyes haunting him. He thought back through everything they had done in class that day, how great she was with Luna and how she wouldn't accept his praise or admit that she was a natural. But more than anything, one phrase she had said stood out to him. One short sentence proved to him she had talent, a gift, for working with horses. He had heard it before, from the greatest girl and horse trainer he had ever known.

The smell of dust and anxious sweat filled the nostrils of twelve-year-old Connor as he slid his hand along the rust-colored rail of the round pen. Inside of the pen, a chocolate-brown mare with a long white stripe running down the center of her face paced the curved fence, screaming for the friends she had left behind when she was put into a horse trailer earlier that morning. Connor's parents, Greg and Jessica Taylor, had gone to an auction and picked her up for his sister, Emily. They didn't know anything about her except that she was a five-year-old thoroughbred mare, but she was showing them that she was nervous, and a little wild.

"Em, we couldn't even get a halter on her to load her in the trailer. We had to back it up to her pen and run her in. That's basically how we unloaded her, too. You need to let your dad go in first," Connor heard his mother explain behind him. He turned away from his place on the fence and saw his sister fold her arms across her chest.

"But she's for me. She's supposed to be mine. I'm not a little kid anymore. I'm sixteen and I know that I can handle this. Why can't you just let me try?" Emily pleaded.

"Because look at her over there. She's running around blind, yelling her head off. You need to let your dad work with her first." Jessica pointed toward the round pen.

Emily turned to her father. "Daddy, please let me work with her. She's supposed to be for me. I need to be the one to establish a bond with her. Not you."

Greg looked from his wife to his daughter, identical gazes staring at him in anticipation. He sighed as he ran a hand through his brown hair. "Jess, she does have a point."

"But it's too dangerous, she could get hurt." Jessica put her hands on her hips.

"We'll be right here. I can step in at any moment if she needs me."

"Which I won't," Emily chimed in.

Connor chuckled at his sister's confidence. Emily turned around at the sound and gave him a wink over her shoulder.

"Alright," their mother said. "But as soon as it looks like she needs help, you're going in."

"Of course." Greg turned to give his daughter instructions, but Emily wasn't staying to listen. She was headed for her new horse.

"Be careful, okay?" Connor murmured as Emily bent down next to him to pick up a lead rope as he opened the gate.

"I will, but you don't need to worry, little brother. She and I are going to be just fine. You'll see."

The gate squeaked as Emily pushed it open and let herself in. The mare jumped and took off to the other side of the pen. Emily walked to the middle of the circle to begin the join-up process. Connor's mom and dad came up behind him and stopped, so they could all watch her work.

"Do you remember how join-up works?" Greg leaned on the fence next to Connor.

"Yeah. She'll move the horse around the circle, getting control of her movement to get her to trust and respect her." Connor's eyes were glued to his sister.

"Yep. And what signs does she look for to see that it's working?"

"The mare will drop her head, she'll lick her lips and chew, and her inside ear should turn toward Emily."

"Very good, kiddo." His mom smiled at him. Connor smiled back at her as they all turned back to Emily and her horse.

Emily stayed patient and kept her body language quiet, doing everything she was supposed to do to encourage the mare to accept her as her leader. She walked a small circle, keeping her focus on the horse working around her. Anytime the mare would whinny or find something else to look at, Emily would ask her to change speeds or go the other way.

The mare was a beautiful mover. She trotted and cantered around Emily with a grace that couldn't be taught. She was listening to Emily's every command but wasn't quite showing the signs of being ready to trust her. She sped up and slowed down and changed direction whenever she was asked, but her head was still up, and her ears were still fixated on everything but Emily.

"Does it normally take this long?" Connor whispered, not wanting to interrupt.

"It takes as long as it takes." His dad whispered back. "Every horse is different. This one looks to be strong-willed, so it may take some time. But don't worry, I'm sure your sister is much more stubborn."

"Yeah, and I wonder where she gets that from." Connor's mother directed her comment toward her husband through a sideways glance.

As they spoke, Emily asked the horse to change directions. Turning, the mare twisted her hind end toward Emily and fired a kick in her direction.

"Greg..." Jessica clutched the rail of the pen, her voice high-pitched with worry.

"It's alright, honey. Look, she's handling it just fine." Emily took charge, reprimanding the mare with her voice and sending her forward with the lead rope.

Jessica sighed uneasily. Emily asked the mare to speed up and slow down and change directions again. The horse started to lower her head. Her ears started rotating, still torn between looking toward the outside world for an escape and finding her reprieve in the girl in the middle of the circle. Emily kept her moving, waiting for the right moment to ask the horse to join her.

With one last change of gait from canter to trot, the mare's ear locked onto Emily. She dropped her nose to the ground and licked her lips, showing the signs of accepting Emily. Knowing this was her opportunity, Emily stepped in front of the horse's shoulder, asking her to stop.

The mare read Emily's body language and responded, halting and turning to face her, a look of hope shining in her big, hazel eyes. Emily turned her back to her, taking any pressure off her and allowing her to make her own decision.

For most people, this part of the join-up was the hardest. It was about patience, waiting for the horse to walk up to them and ask to be their partner. But it was also about knowing when you had waited too long, when it hadn't worked, and when it was time to send the horse back out to the rail.

Connor's eyes alternated between his sister and her horse. Emily was staring at the ground, being careful not to move. The mare was staring at Emily's back, and Connor could read the debate going on in her mind through her body language. She wanted Emily, but she also wanted her freedom.

Emily's fingers twitched on the lead rope. Her eyes lifted and met Connor's as she struggled with making the decision to wait or to put the mare back in motion. Emily's shoulders lifted as she sighed. Connor noticed the slightest shift of her foot as she began to turn around, but she paused at just the right second. The horse was walking to her.

Emily again stood motionless. The mare walked right to her and lifted her head to smell Emily's, the color of her muzzle and coat matching Emily's hair. Emily smiled as the mare's breath tickled the back of her neck. Without turning to face her, she reached up and touched the mare's white nose with one finger. The horse didn't run or flinch, accepting Emily's stroke.

Emily moved forward, to see if she would follow her. The mare hesitated, but then took a few steps to catch up. When she stopped, Emily turned, taking her time, not wanting to startle her. This time when she reached out, she rubbed her shoulder. The horse turned her head toward her with kind eyes. Their partnership had been established.

"Great job, Em. That was beautiful." Jessica wiped at tears in her eyes.

"It was, sweetie. I couldn't have done it better." Greg put his arm around his wife's shoulders.

"That was pretty cool," Connor added, causing everyone to laugh.

"Thanks, guys." Emily continued petting the mare. "But it wasn't me. It was all her."

A rumble of monsoon thunder and a sudden gust of wind evaporated the memory and brought Connor back to his truck. The first few cold drops of rain hit his arm through the open window. He put his keys in the ignition and rolled up the windows as he pulled out of the parking lot and away from the farm. Sniffing and swallowing hard as he turned into traffic, he forced the lump of tears building inside his throat to subside. He needed to concentrate on driving home.

Six

THE SUNBAKED METAL BLEACHERS STARTED TO BURN the back of Caroline's thighs through her shorts, forcing her to turn and adjust the faded red beach towel she was sitting on. All around her, fans focused on the first fall baseball game, and her former teammates were busy chatting about their classes, their own upcoming games, and the guys on the baseball team. Caroline heard bits and pieces of each conversation but struggled to participate beyond a nod or a smile here and there. Her mind was about four miles away, stuck down the road at the U of A farm in the weanling class.

Monday would be her first practical with Luna.

The filly was coming along well. During the past two weeks, Caroline and Connor had taught her how to walk on a lead line. Luna had been fussy at first, but they had gotten through it. She was now leading very well and would walk right next to either of her handlers. She could also halt when asked and back up a few steps, but there were still moments when Luna's stubborn side would show up. She would sometimes stop and try to turn away from them or would speed up and try to take off. Luna wasn't misbehaving or being naughty; she was just still testing her boundaries, like most young horses.

Caroline knew that Luna wasn't being mean, but it still scared her quite a bit when she would act like that. She would do her best to discipline the filly but would hand her over to Connor as soon as she could. Connor had been a great help and seemed to be learning when she needed him to step in. In the last couple of classes, she hadn't even had to say anything. He had just come up and offered to take Luna, giving Caroline a break. Having Connor as her partner was the only reason she had made it this far in the course. He was helping her feel safe, and that made her want to trust him.

But she wouldn't have Connor's help during the practical. They were going to be graded as individuals, each taking a turn with Luna, showing how she could walk, halt, and back up when asked. If Luna acted up in the middle of Caroline's turn, it would be up to her to deal with it, and she wasn't sure she was ready. Or if she ever would be.

"Caroline, did you hear me?" Vanessa Lewis, a third baseman she had played with since high school, waved her hand in front of Caroline's face.

She blinked and shook her head. "Oh, no, I'm sorry, I didn't. What's up?"

"I just said Ryan's on deck. If he gets a homerun, he'll have hit for the cycle. Where were you?"

"Just lost in thought, I guess. I hope he gets it. He's been working really hard." Caroline looked toward the on-deck circle. Ryan had already had a great game. He had hit three for three, with a single, a double, and a triple. A homerun here would mean he accomplished something very few players could.

"Is he still getting calls from scouts?" Vanessa adjusted the part of the towel she was sitting on.

"Yeah, here and there. They've been letting him know they're watching his numbers and that they like what they see. He's pretty thrilled about it."

"He should be. That's pretty exciting."

"It is." Caroline worked to keep a cheery tone in her voice.

Vanessa studied her for a moment. "But it can't be easy on you."

Caroline sighed and reached up to tighten her ponytail, buying time as she tried to come up with an answer to dismiss Vanessa's statement. She looked back at her friend, but no words came. She just nodded her head in agreement.

Vanessa seemed to understand. "Are you guys okay? Do you tell him it's hard?"

"We're okay for the most part. He's so happy and things are going so well for him that he doesn't get what it's like for me. I don't want to take away from what he's got going on, so I don't talk about myself much. For his sake and for mine."

"I can understand that." Vanessa reached over and squeezed Caroline's arm. "Well, just know if you ever do need to talk about anything, you've always got me."

"Thanks, girl. I appreciate it."

"Anytime."

Both of them turned their attention back to the field as the batter in front of Ryan reached base with a single. Ryan walked up to the left-handed batter's box and prepared for his chance to hit. The crowd grew almost silent, knowing what was at stake.

Caroline held her breath as the opposing pitcher received the signal from the catcher and delivered the first pitch. The ball snapped into the glove, high out of the strike zone. The ump called ball one. The next pitch was pretty much the same and was called for ball two. The catcher called time out and jogged out to the mound.

"They're not gonna give him anything to hit," Vanessa whispered.

"Maybe they will," Caroline uttered back.

The catcher hustled back to home plate and got back down in his crouch. Caroline watched the pitcher nod, agreeing to the pitch, before stepping toward home plate. She could tell the ball was in the strike zone a second before Ryan swung. The pop of the bat as it made contact with the ball was all the crowd needed to hear to know it was out of the park. Caroline's eyes followed the ball as it flew out over the fence in the gap between center field and right field.

The fans hopped to their feet, cheering and stomping. Ryan's teammates rushed out of the dugout, falling over each other in the rush to meet their hero. Stepping on third base, he high-fived his coach and sprinted into the huddle waiting for him at home plate. The guys jumped up and down, pounding him on his helmet and back.

As the celebration dwindled, Caroline looked toward the mound. The pitcher's shoulders were slumped, and he was staring at the dirt, kicking himself over how he had thrown that pitch. Even if it was a team sport, pitcher was a lonely position. Wins and losses were recorded by your name alone, and you controlled whether or not the ball stayed in or left the park. Caroline knew that thrill, and that sense of defeat, all too well.

"Ryan Cole! Ryan Cole!" The chant echoed throughout the field as the crowd encouraged Ryan to come back out of the dugout for an encore. His sweaty blond head appeared, and he tipped his helmet toward the fans, thanking them for their encouragement. Everyone applauded and cheered.

Caroline could see Ryan searching the crowd, and she knew he was looking for her. Their eyes met, and he gave her a big smile. Doing her best to smile, she gave him a small thumbs-up.

As he went back down to the dugout, Vanessa elbowed her. "Even if he can't understand what you're going through, it's pretty clear he's still crazy about you. He just hit for the cycle and thousands of people are up here screaming his name, and he only wanted to find you."

"I know." Caroline took a deep breath. "That's what I'm holding on to."

The batter after Ryan hit a pop-up to the second baseman, ending the home half of the inning. Ryan and his teammates jogged back out to the field to their defensive positions. They were three outs away from winning, six runs to two.

Caroline watched as Ryan took his warm-up grounders and noticed his focus and intensity, his passion for the game. These were the attributes that had made her fall for him all those years ago. These were the same attributes they had had in common.

The inning was easy, three up, three down. As the teams on the field shook hands, the softball girls started getting up and moving around. Caroline stood with them and stretched.

"We're gonna go eat in the union, if you wanna come?" Vanessa put her bag over her shoulder.

"I better wait for Ryan. I think he wanted to do something, but I'll let you know for sure in a little bit." Caroline's eyes followed Ryan as he walked to the dugout. A few of his buddies slapped him on the back as they went, laughing and joking.

Vanessa glanced down to where Caroline was looking.

She cleared her throat, forcing Caroline to look at her. "Try not to take it personally if he goes out with those guys instead of you. He had kind of a big day."

"Yeah, I know. I'll do my best." Caroline sighed. "You guys have fun."

Caroline turned and walked down the steps of the bleachers, heading in the opposite direction of her friends. She found a small bench near the exit of the dugout and sat down to wait.

Her mind drifted to Luna and the practical that was staring her down. She knew the steps she should follow if the filly acted up, but it was putting them into action that caused her to freeze. Anytime the young horse needed discipline, Luna would resist. The look on her face reminded Caroline too much of Beau.

Maybe it was because they were brother and sister.

Caroline had been drawn to Stellar's picture in the entryway that first day at the farm. The photo of the dark stallion, back in his prime when he won race after race, was one she had seen before. She knew everything about him, since Beau had been from his first crop of babies. Beau hadn't been much of a racehorse. He'd made only two starts and had finished close to last in both of them. He had come to her mother for training straight off the track. It didn't take long to teach him how to jump or do dressage, as he was willing and talented. He won almost every three-day event he competed in and had taken Caroline to the Young Rider Championships. Beau had been a dapple gray, taking after his mother, but his face and eyes were the same as his father's. The same as Luna's.

In class, she tried not to think about the fact that Luna was related to Beau, connecting the filly to her past, but some days it haunted her more than anything. They were so alike in how they moved and acted.

"There's my girl!" Ryan exclaimed as he came out from the dugout. Caroline stood, sending away the images that were dancing in front of her, and put a smile on her face.

"Ryan, that was incredible. I'm so happy for you." Caroline spoke into his shoulder as he pulled her into a hug.

He stepped back and took both of her hands in his, his eyes sparkling. "I'm the first one on this team to do it in ten years. I really thought they weren't going to pitch to me that last at bat. But then I saw that fastball right where I wanted it. I couldn't have asked for a better pitch," he rambled, squeezing her fingers.

"Hey, Ryan, come on, we're taking you out to celebrate, man," one of Ryan's teammates yelled before Caroline could say anything.

Ryan looked at Caroline, his green eyes reflecting her face back at her.

"It's okay if you want to go with them," she muttered. "It was a big day. I get it."

Ryan opened his mouth to answer his buddies without taking his gaze off Caroline. "Some other time, guys. I've got plans."

Caroline didn't have to fake her smile this time. As his teammates laughed at him and made jokes about him picking her over them, he bent down and gave her a quick, soft kiss.

"Come on, let's go eat."

"Sounds good to me," she nodded as he turned, keeping ahold of one of her hands and leading her toward the union.

As they walked, he began telling her about every pitch he had seen and which ones he had hit on his way to the cycle. Her smile faded a little, as she was once again reminded of the different places they were now at in their lives. Every dream Ryan had ever had was coming true, while she was struggling to find something to pursue, something to believe in. No matter how happy she was for him, it still hurt her heart when she thought about it.

But what hurt more was that Ryan still didn't seem to notice. He kept talking as she leaned against his arm, not realizing how quiet she had become. But every few sentences, he would squeeze her hand. It was a simple action, a small display of affection, and it reassured her that he still cared for her. Maybe his success hadn't blinded him or made him forget what she was going through.

And as she had told Vanessa, that hope was all she had to hold on to.

Seven

"EASY, GIRL," CONNOR MURMURED IN A QUIET TONE as he clutched the lead rope, trying to keep Jewel, the broodmare his dad was vaccinating, from moving around too much. They had been vaccinating for most of the afternoon, and the horses were starting to anticipate the pokes of the needle.

The mare's copper coat glistened as her muscles went rigid underneath her skin. Greg Taylor rubbed her neck, being patient as he waited for her to relax. Jewel dropped her head with a sigh, and in one fluid motion, Greg injected the drug. The mare didn't flinch.

"Thatta girl, Jewel." Connor patted her neck before taking the halter off, freeing her to go back to her friends in the pasture. "Who's left?"

Greg looked at his clipboard, grasping the corner of the page as he studied the list of horses. "Looks like all we have left is Dream."

Connor looked out across the pasture, where a light breeze ruffled the yellowing grass, searching for the milk-chocolate mare. He found her by the large stock tank, using her nose to splash herself with the cool water. It was easy to see she had been at it for a while, as a large mud puddle had formed around the edges of the tank. Connor sighed and began the trek across the grass.

"Hope you're ready to get wet," his dad chuckled as he prepared the vaccine.

"Always." Connor rolled his eyes. He walked to the edge of Dream's puddle, then stopped. "Hey, pretty girl. Why don't you come see me?"

Dream lifted her head, nickering at him as she took a few steps in his direction.

"That's my girl." Connor lifted his hand toward the mare, encouraging her to keep coming to him. But Dream had other plans and stopped to paw in the mud, splattering Connor from head to toe.

"Ah, Dream! That's not nice!" Connor yelled as he turned away.

"I guess I should have said 'hope you're ready to get muddy,'" Greg managed to call out between his rounds of laughter.

"Yeah, no kidding." Connor wiped his face with the back of his hand. He felt hot air on the back of his neck and turned to see that Dream had come up behind him. She bounced her head up and down, as if she was eyeing her work with the mud.

"You're pretty happy with yourself, aren't you?" Connor reached over the mare's ears to buckle the halter. Dream snorted and rubbed her head on his shoulder. "Yeah, yeah, yeah, let's go." Together they walked toward his dad.

Weeks had passed since the memory of Emily had played out in his truck, but he still hadn't been able to shake it, to shake her. He couldn't seem to put a lid on that box, and walking Emily's horse, covered with mud, brought back another scene of his sister. He blinked to stop the image forming in front of him and discovered the wetness that had developed behind his eyes.

Connor cleared his throat, working to hide his feelings

from his dad. But when he looked up, his dad's eyes reflected the same emotion he was trying to hide.

"You know what this reminds me of?" Greg reached out to pat the mare on her shoulder.

"Her first cross-country practice with Em?" Connor guessed.

"Oh, yeah. Em was so worried about whether or not Dream would go in the water. Little did she know she would leap in, paw like crazy, and soak both of them. Ever since then, this girl has always played in whatever water she could find." Greg rubbed Dream behind her ears.

"We all thought she'd hesitate, but no. She'd do anything for Emily." Connor looked down at the ground as he spoke, pulling at a loose strand of string coming off the lead rope.

"Yeah, she would." Greg coughed. "Alright, sweet mare, time for a little poke. Then you can go back to your swimming hole."

Connor refocused on Dream, to make sure she held still while she got her shot. Dream didn't even acknowledge the needle, enjoying the attention she was getting. "Such a perfect girl." Connor leaned his forehead into her soft cheek.

Greg disposed of the needle and syringe and turned back to the mare. "Yeah, she is pretty perfect." He rubbed the mare in the center of her forehead with his fingertips, sending shedding white hairs from her long blaze into the wind. Dropping his hand, he turned to Connor. "She's all set, and we're all done. You can let her go." He bent down to gather his clipboard and the plastic tote he'd brought the vaccines out with.

Connor looked into Dream's gentle eye and gave her nose one last stroke. "Have fun, little missy," he told her, unbuckling the halter. He watched as Dream trotted right back to the water tank, noticing how her belly was widening, beginning to show the foal she would give birth to in another five months.

"Dream is starting to get a baby belly." His dad held the gate open for him. "She'll be such a good mom."

"Yeah, she will. That baby should be pretty, too." Greg clicked his pen closed and put it in his shirt pocket. "We've been busy the last couple of weeks. I haven't had much of a chance to talk to you. How's school? How's the weanling class?"

"School's good, and the weanling class is great. By far my favorite class. Dr. Carnes is pretty cool, very knowledgeable. The horses and the farm are impressive," he replied in one breath.

"Do you like your weanling?"

"Yeah, her name is Luna. She's a thoroughbred, a little bit of a diva, which can be challenging sometimes. She's put together really well. Here, I can show you." Connor reached into the pocket of his jeans and pulled out his phone. His finger slid across the screen as he went through his photos, searching for the one of him with Luna and Caroline they had taken in class last week. He tapped to make it bigger, then handed it to his dad.

Greg studied the filly for a moment. "Wow, she is pretty. Look at her shoulder and her neck conformation. Just about perfect. I've never seen such a dark-black bay. Is that a crescent moon on her head?"

"Yeah, I think that's why they called her Luna."

"It fits her." Greg examined the picture for another few seconds before handing the phone back to Connor with a wide grin on his face. "The girl is pretty too. Who's she?"

Connor felt heat in his cheeks even though he tried to

control his reaction. "My partner for the class, Caroline Davis."

"Doug and Holly's daughter?" Surprise clouded Greg's expression. "I thought she quit horses after the accident?"

"She did. From what I can tell, she hasn't been around horses until this class started. I'm not sure why she's taking it."

"Did you ask her? Or tell her who you are?"

"No, I didn't. On the first day of class, Dr. Carnes told me he partnered her with me because she has no prior experience. He wanted me to help her out. I figured if she's lying about her past, she doesn't need me asking too many questions, or telling her I know who she is." Connor shrugged his shoulders, leaning back on the pasture fence.

"I wonder why she'd lie, though." Greg pinched his eyebrows together, as he moved to lean next to Connor.

"It's probably easier. Then she doesn't have to explain to everyone what happened, or that she quit. I think she's just trying to save herself from any pain the truth could cause her."

Greg nodded his head at Connor's words. "How is she with Luna?"

"She's amazing," Connor breathed. "I mean, when she manages to put her fear aside, she's incredible. She's a natural, and talented. I wish I had her instincts."

"You like her." Greg elbowed Connor's side.

"I want to help her." Connor ignored his dad's lighthearted teasing. "She reminds me of Emily." He dropped his eyes, studying the toes of his boots. "The other day, she got Luna's halter on her for the first time. Luna started to fight her, but Caroline was perfect. She stayed with her, stayed patient. When I tried to compliment her on it, she wouldn't take it. She told me it wasn't her, that it was all Luna."

Connor heard his dad inhale and looked up to see his eyes. Greg blinked several times before he spoke. "Yeah, that sounds like Emily."

"I know, right? But she gets so worried, even when things are going just fine. I don't know what to do for her."

"I think you just keep doing what you're doing. Like you said, there's a reason she's hiding. Just be her friend, be supportive."

Connor sighed. "It doesn't feel like enough sometimes."

Greg grasped Connor's shoulder. "Well, there is one other thing you can do. The most important thing. We can even do it right now."

"What's that?"

"We can pray for her." Greg closed his eyes as Connor nodded in agreement and followed his dad's lead. "God, we want to lift up Caroline to You. You know the journey she has been on to bring her into Connor's life and to the weanling class. Please show Connor how to be the friend she needs." Greg paused, collecting his thoughts. "And Lord, if You could, say hi to our Emily for us. We miss her, and we've been thinking about her a lot today." Greg swallowed. "In Jesus's name, amen."

"Amen," Connor echoed as his dad squeezed his shoulder. He lifted his lips in a small smile. "Thanks, Dad."

"Anytime, buddy. Come on, your mom is probably wondering where we are."

They walked in silence past the barns to the winding stone path that led to the house. They climbed the steps to the white porch, and Connor fingered the vines of ivy that wrapped around the railing. The creaking screen door announced their presence as Connor followed his dad inside.

"Greg? Connor?" his mother's voice called from the kitchen.

"It's us." Greg sat down on the bench in the entryway to take of his boots, scooting over to make room for Connor to join him.

"Connor Jacob!" Jessica Taylor gasped. "Don't you even think about taking another step into this house like that! What happened to you?"

Connor froze, confused by his mom's tone. His dad started laughing, and Connor switched his eyes back and forth between his parents. Jessica was squinting at him, moving her glare from his shirt to his pants.

"Dream happened." Greg stood up, put an arm around his wife with a quick kiss on her cheek, and joined her in staring at their son. Connor looked down and remembered he had taken a mud bath.

"Oh, right. Dream thought I needed a mud facial, but she didn't stop at just my face." He grinned at his mom. "I'll go straight to my room to change. It's pretty much dry. I don't think I'll get it on anything." Before she could send him out to the barn to hose off and change in the wash rack, he bolted up the stairs.

"You better not! Or you'll be scrubbing the floors!" Connor could hear her laughing through her threat.

The door to his room shut with a click. Squeaking open the door to his closet, he found a clean t-shirt and a clean pair of jeans. He peeled off the muddy shirt and pants and pulled on the new ones. Gathering the dirty stuff up in his arms, he examined the floor, making sure no dried mud had been left on his carpet.

Once he was sure the floor was clean, he stood and headed with his muddy mess to the washing machine. His eyes fell on a picture of his sister and him with Dream, after their first competition together. The blue ribbon clipped onto Dream's bridle matched the shining blue of his sister's eyes. She had the largest smile on her face. Connor had been so proud of them, and his smile was just as big.

He tore his eyes from the picture and forced himself to walk down the hall, away from the reminder of how life could change as quick as a lightning strike. Away from the ache of missing Emily.

He couldn't do anything to bring Emily back, to make more memories with her. All he could do was remember her and treasure the connection they still had through Dream. Putting his clothes in the washer, he realized there was one other thing he could do to help keep his sister with him.

He could help Caroline overcome her fear and face whatever truth she was hiding from.

Eight

THE PATTERN WAS SIMPLE ENOUGH. Four orange traffic cones were laid out in a straight line. All Caroline had to do was walk Luna from cone one to two, trot her from two to three, walk from three to four, then halt and back up five steps. It was an easier practical than she had been picturing. There were no turns or other requirements that would make it tricky. But there was one thing that had kicked her anxiety up a few notches, one thing that would make Luna, and all the babies in class, much more likely to misbehave.

The wind was blowing twenty-five miles an hour.

Caroline's shirt whipped around her as she worked to keep her eyes open through the dust to see Connor and Luna. Connor was up next to do his practical. His light-brown hair flipped over his head as the wind pushed against it. The muscles in his forearm were taut as he led Luna around at the walk, pausing every few moments to ask her to halt and back up. The filly was doing her best to stay focused, but the spooking and spinning antics of her friends were making it difficult for her.

"Connor?" Dr. Carnes looked up from his clipboard as Laura finished her pattern with Rebel. The colt was going through a growth spurt and towered over the other weanlings. As Connor passed Laura and Rebel, leading Luna to the first cone, a gust of wind knocked it over. Rebel squealed and leapt up off the ground, kicking his hind legs behind him at the cone. Luna spun in response, afraid that the large colt was coming after her.

"Whoa, Luna, you're alright." Connor tightened his grip on the lead rope and circled the filly. As Rebel arched his neck and pranced away from her, Luna stopped, but kept her head high and her eyes on Rebel. Caroline reminded herself to breathe.

"Connor, you can have a minute if you want. Make sure her attention is back on you." Dr. Carnes moved to reset the cone.

"Thank you." Connor turned and walked Luna a few steps, then asked her to trot. She did everything he asked. He turned her back and made eye contact with Caroline.

"We're okay. Nothing like a little wind to make things a bit more interesting." Stopping Luna next to Caroline, Connor smiled at his partner.

Caroline studied Connor's eyes but found no trace of the fear or concern she was feeling, even after what had just happened. She pressed her lips together and nodded her head, the one way she was able to acknowledge that Connor had spoken to her. Luna pulled against the lead rope to reach for Caroline. Caroline stiffened but lifted her hand to stroke the filly on her nose.

"Ready, Connor?" Dr. Carnes clicked his pen as he wrote Connor's name on the practical rubric.

"Be good, little one." Caroline whispered as she dropped her hand. She crossed her arms over her midsection, locking her eyes on Connor's back as he led Luna a few paces away from where they had been standing. He gave Luna one last sideways glance before he looked straight ahead and began the pattern.

Luna walked from the first cone to the second like an

angel. Her steps were in sync with Connor, the hold on the lead rope light, as it should be. As they reached the second cone, Connor increased his speed, prompting the filly to trot. She bounded forward, her tail arching over her back as another gust of wind kicked up the dust. Connor steadied her and continued on with the pattern. They went back down to the walk, stopped, and backed up, finishing the practical without any extra excitement. Connor rubbed Luna on her shoulder, praising her for staying with him throughout the practical.

"Well done, Connor." Dr. Carnes looked up at Caroline as he spoke. "I have five to go, then it'll be your turn, alright?"

Caroline's throat went dry as she opened her mouth to respond to her teacher. Again, no words formed, but she managed to nod her head once. Dr. Carnes turned to call on the next student as Connor brought her Luna.

You can do this. Just breathe. She clenched her fists together, trying to steady herself before she took the lead rope. As her fingers touched the cotton, her stomach dropped, and she thought she might throw up.

"Hey, are you okay? You're as white as a lily." Connor kept one hand on Luna's lead.

"I'm not sure I can do this." Caroline gulped as she stared down at her boots.

"I think you can." Connor placed his hand on the back of hers, forcing Caroline to look up at him. "Just walk her around for a few minutes before you have to go. I'll be here if you need anything."

"You sure?"

"Yes. You'll be fine. Don't even think about the wind, alright? Just think about leading her. It'll be great."

"Alright, I'll try."

"Thatta girl."

Connor let go of the lead as Caroline took Luna. She ran her fingers through her short black forelock and took a deep breath, pushing the air out of her mouth in a rush. She turned and led Luna a few yards away before she asked her to halt. She pivoted around to face the filly and asked her to back up. Luna listened to the cue, doing what she was told without hesitation. Caroline took another deep breath as she asked her to trot. Again, the filly sped up without misbehaving.

Caroline slowed her step and walked back to Connor. He was smiling at her, but she wasn't feeling enough relief to smile back. She still had to get through the practical. She still had to deal with the wind.

"That was perfect. I told you it would be fine." Connor rubbed Luna's crescent moon as he looked at Caroline. Caroline wished she could feel the confidence that shone through his rich brown eyes.

Another gust came through the field, whistling through the grass and vibrating the wires of the field fencing. Caroline tensed as Luna did, but the filly stood still. Caroline gazed at Connor with doubt.

"See? She didn't do anything. The only reason she did earlier was because of Rebel. And besides, she got it all out of her system with me." Connor shrugged his shoulders and grinned at her.

"I hope so." Caroline lifted one side of her mouth, trying to joke back at him.

"Caroline? Are you ready?" Dr. Carnes searched the pasture.

She nodded her head. "Here goes nothing." She led Luna toward the first cone.

Connor fell into step with her. "Remember what I said,

don't think about the wind. Lead her like you just did and it'll be over before you know it."

Caroline didn't answer as she focused on the cone getting closer with each step. *Just one foot in front of the other. That's all we have to do.*

That thought carried their steps to the second cone. Just as Caroline began to ask Luna to trot, the wind howled, lifting Luna's mane straight off her neck. The filly's head went straight up in the air as she screeched to a halt. Caroline turned, finding Luna's gaze locked onto something behind her. The whites of her eyes showed around the black, expressing fear. Caroline looked to see what she was staring at.

The dumpster across the parking lot had blown open. Pieces of trash were racing through the air. A plastic shopping bag was rattling its way straight for Luna.

Caroline froze as the bag dove down and crinkled against Luna's hind legs. The filly spun around. Caroline gave the rope a quick tug, but it was too late. Luna reared, standing up on her hind legs, pawing the air inches above Caroline's head with her front hooves.

Caroline worked to keep ahold of the lead, as the cotton pulled and burned across the palms of her hands. She stepped to the side of Luna, as she had been taught, to get out of the way of the striking hooves. She could see Dr. Carnes and Connor coming toward her, but there wasn't much they could do to help.

"Luna, it's okay. You're alright." Caroline tried to soothe the horse as tears threatened to spill down her face. "Please, Luna."

The filly lowered her front end back to the ground. Her eyes rolled around as she searched for the plastic bag, careening her neck in every direction. Luna looked so much like Beau had in his final moments, causing Caroline's heart to ache.

"Caroline, here let me take her." Connor strode to her, his hands already extended to grab the lead rope.

Luna jumped sideways at the suddenness of Connor's movements, still startled from the trauma of the bag. Caroline put a hand on her shoulder to calm her, but the filly trembled under her hand.

"Shhh, little girl, easy now. We aren't gonna hurt you." Caroline rubbed Luna with just the tips of her fingers, encouraging her muscles to relax.

"Caroline?"

"I'm okay, Connor. Give us a minute." She never took her eyes off Luna and never stopped circling her fingers over her shoulder, waiting for the filly to calm down.

Luna eyed Caroline with suspicion, but as the seconds passed, she leaned into her touch. She dropped her head and licked her lips with a gentle sigh, relieved that the trauma was over.

"Um, Dr. Carnes?" Caroline called out as she continued to soothe Luna. "Do you want me to start over?"

Connor and the instructor tried to hide their surprise that Caroline was ready to continue with the practical. Dr. Carnes glanced down at his clipboard as he cleared his throat. "No, that's alright. If you just want to get her back in line with the second cone, you can pick up the trot and go on from there. But if you want, you can have a few minutes to refocus."

Caroline bit her lip as she studied Luna. The filly was standing still, enjoying the attention she was getting. Caroline felt Connor just a few steps behind her and could sense how he was ready to jump in and take Luna from her. But she knew if she handed her over before completing her practical, she wouldn't be able to take her back. The last thing she needed was time to refocus, or time to think about what had happened.

"I think we'll just go for it, if that's okay?" She gave Luna a final pat as she turned her back toward the cones.

"Of course." Dr. Carnes and Connor walked to the starting point of the pattern.

Caroline paused a few steps from the second cone. Luna halted right next to her. "Okay, little one, let's try this again. One step at a time, alright?"

Their steps found a rhythm as they closed the distance between them and the second cone. Passing it, Caroline lengthened her stride and clucked, asking Luna to trot. The filly's stride extended to match her handler's, as she picked up the smooth and gentle gait. They covered the ground to the third cone in no time and slowed back down to the walk. Reaching the final cone, they halted in sync. Caroline turned, and Luna backed up right away, listening to the last request Caroline gave her as if the bag had never even touched her.

"Good girl, Luna." Caroline gave her a scratch on the neck before heading back toward Connor and Dr. Carnes.

"That was very well done, Caroline. I'm impressed. Not many students would have opted to continue after dealing with all of that."

Caroline shrugged. "Thank you, sir."

Dr. Carnes nodded before he began looking for the next student to complete their practical.

Caroline let her eyes find Connor's. His expression showed a mixture of awe and worry. Caroline gave him a half smile. "You can take her now if you want. I don't think she'll do anything now. She definitely got it all out of her system with me."

Connor paused before he laughed, realizing she had turned his joke from earlier around back on him. He stepped up and took the lead rope out of her hands. "Yeah, I guess she did."

As her hands relaxed from the hold she had on Luna, Caroline felt the sting of the rope burn set in across her skin. She looked down and saw angry red lines beginning to show across her palms.

"Rope burn?" Connor leaned in closer to get a look.

Caroline closed her fists and dropped them to her side. "Yeah, but not too bad. I've certainly had worse."

"You have?" Connor's face was curious.

"Um, yeah." Caroline stuttered. "Ride...I mean, playing softball, you can get pretty beat up." Swallowing, she hoped Connor wouldn't pick up on what she had almost said.

"I thought you were just a manager?"

"I am. I used to play." Caroline pressed her lips together. It was the first time she had said this out loud.

"Time to wrap it up. I think we've had enough excitement for one day," Dr. Carnes announced, interrupting Connor as he opened his mouth to ask another question.

"Behave yourself, little missy." Caroline cupped her hands around Luna's muzzle. The filly blew warm air across the rope burn. "I know you didn't mean to do it," she whispered into her fuzzy ears.

She took a step back as Connor took off her halter. Walking toward the gate, the image of Luna's face when she looked like Beau flooded Caroline's mind. Tears welled up in her eyes as the ache in her took hold again.

"Caroline, do your hands hurt that bad? You look like you're gonna cry." Connor touched her shoulder.

She shook her head, dismissing his concern and her memory in one quick action. "No, I'm fine. It's just the wind irritating my eyes."

"Are you sure?"

"Yep, they hardly sting anymore. I'm good." They entered the classroom and picked up their backpacks before heading to the parking lot.

Connor stopped as they reached Caroline's car. "I'd put something on your hands when you get home, even if they aren't that bad." Connor glanced down toward them as he spoke.

"I will. I promise."

"Good. Well, I'll see you Wednesday." Connor smiled, then headed toward his truck.

"See you then." Caroline unlocked her car door and pulled it open, fighting the wind as it tried to rip it out of her hands. She slid in and slammed it shut.

Shaking, she was unsettled by what had happened with Luna and how close she had come to accidentally telling Connor about riding. How close she had come to actually saying it out loud.

She turned her hands over in her lap. The burns still stung, but the pain she felt from them was nothing compared to the hurt she felt inside her chest. She hadn't missed Beau like this in a long time, and she wasn't sure how to move past it.

Caroline let the image of Luna play out in front of her. She held her breath as the familiar terror grasped her stomach and closed off her throat. As the scene continued, the dark bay filly turned into a large gray gelding. He wasn't rearing but was lying on his side, fighting to get up. The emotions she felt coming from the horse matched the ones holding her hostage.

Another gust of wind blew dust into her window, rattling the image from her mind. She started the car, pulled into the line of traffic leaving the farm, and did her best to focus on the bumper in front of her.

Nine

THE VIBRATIONS OF VOICES AND FOOTSTEPS added to the chaos of the student union. The wind of the day before had brought rain from a tropical storm in Mexico, forcing the students who liked to eat lunch in the open air to come inside. The tables were jam packed, and Connor couldn't find a place to sit. He clutched the brown paper Burger King sack in his fist as yet another person collided with him.

He sighed and shook it off, lifting his eyes above the jostling heads as he searched for somewhere he could eat. He turned the corner into the last section of seating and saw an empty seat at a high-top table for two. The girl sitting there was hovering over a textbook, a pen curled in her hand. Her foot and her head bounced up and down in rhythm with the music from her headphones. As she threw her blond hair over her shoulder, Connor recognized her. He worked his way through the crowd to the edge of the table.

"Caroline? Can I sit here?" Connor grasped the top of the chair with his free hand. Caroline kept her eyes down on the book in front of her, not hearing him over the noise in the union or her headphones. Connor went ahead and scooted the empty chair out, tossing his lunch sack on the table and slinging his backpack off his shoulder and over the side of the chair.

Caroline dropped her pen as she jumped, startled by the motion in front of her. She reached up to pull her headphones out.

Connor paused. "I'm sorry. I didn't mean to surprise you. I asked if I could sit here, but you didn't hear me." Connor pointed to her headphones. "There's nowhere else to sit. You aren't waiting on anyone, are you?"

"Oh, no, I'm not. Go ahead. Sorry I didn't hear you. I was a little wrapped up in chemistry." Caroline closed the textbook, leaving her pen in it to mark her page.

"Chemistry or the private concert you had going on in your head?" Connor teased as he sat down. "To me, it looked like you were having more of a dance party than a study session."

Caroline's cheeks turned from their normal light pink to a deeper shade of red. She folded her hands in her lap as she sat back in her chair. "Maybe you should eat your lunch before it gets too cold."

"Yeah, you're probably right." Connor grinned as he pulled his burger, fries, and a few napkins out of the bag. He closed his eyes and bowed his head.

Lord, thank you for the rain. I know it's caused the union to be extra crowded and obnoxious today, but we need the rain here in the desert. It's also allowed me this chance to sit with Caroline, so please show me how to be a friend to her. And thank you for this food that I am about to eat. In Your name I pray, Amen.

Connor lifted his eyes as he unwrapped his burger. Caroline was staring at him, her expression one of curiosity and sadness.

"You're a Christian?"

"Yes, I am. What about you?" Connor picked up his food and took a bite.

"Used to be." Caroline shrugged her shoulders as she tilted her head and smiled with half of her mouth.

Connor thought about her statement as he chewed, trying to figure out how to respond. He swallowed. "Used to be," he repeated. "Do you want to explain that?"

Caroline sighed and rested her chin in her hand as she looked out over the sea of students in the union. When she looked back at him, Connor could sense the pain coming off her. "It's a long story. Some other time, maybe."

Connor could tell he shouldn't push her. "Alright, some other time then."

"Thanks."

"No problem."

Connor took another few bites in silence, considering where to take the conversation. He studied the navy polo shirt she was wearing, focusing on the red and white block-type A with "Arizona Softball" typed out underneath it.

Caroline snapped her head down. "Do I have something on my shirt?" She stretched it out in front of her, examining it.

Connor blinked as he realized he had been staring. "Oh, no, you don't. Sorry. I was just looking at the embroidery. I was wondering about you and softball."

Caroline let go of the material. "What do you want to know?"

"Well, you said you're the manager for the team, but yesterday you told me you used to play. I guess I'm wondering why you stopped?"

"That's another long story."

"I've got time." Connor smiled at her as he picked up a fry.

Caroline eyed him, carefulness and hesitation showing on her face. Sighing, she ran her hand through her bangs.

"On one condition."

"What's that?"

"I get to have a couple of fries."

Connor scooted the white cardboard container toward her and handed her a napkin. "Go for it."

Caroline took a few fries and set them down on the napkin. "Alright. So, my dad was a professional baseball pitcher, won a World Series with the Diamondbacks and everything. It's because of him that I started playing when I was five and started pitching when I was eight."

"Daddy's little girl?" Connor questioned as Caroline paused to eat a fry.

"Yeah, I guess so. I was pretty good, and I enjoyed it, but I only played in the city league during the summers. I didn't really start to focus on it until after the accid...I mean, until I was a sophomore in high school. I threw a no-hitter in the state championship game that year." A wide smile spread across her face, causing her blue eyes to sparkle.

"Wow, that's awesome." Connor realized it was the first time a smile had ever reached her eyes in the weeks they had been working together.

"Thanks." Her smile stayed in place. "It was after that game that I got invited to play with one of the best travel ball teams in the state. I started going to tournaments every weekend and had my first unofficial scholarship offer by the beginning of my junior year."

"You got more than one offer?" Connor interrupted.

"Yep. I actually received four official offers. UCLA, Washington, Florida, and Arizona."

"Whoa." Connor was impressed. He didn't know much about sports, but he knew that this was a big deal, that all of her offers came from big schools. "I'm guessing you chose Arizona?"

"Yeah, it was an easy choice. Tucson is my hometown. I grew up going to Arizona games, and the program here is kind of a legacy. I couldn't pass up the opportunity to be a part of it." Caroline stopped to put another fry in her mouth.

"What happened then?" Connor finished his burger and crumbled the wrapper up, tossing it into the empty bag.

Caroline exhaled. "I had a great freshman year. We went undefeated in the fall season, and in non-conference play. We had just one loss in Pac-12 play with me pitching. I was named Pac-12 Freshman of the Year. I was a top ten finalist for National Player of the Year. We went to the College World Series, and I dominated. I didn't give up a run in three games, sending us straight to the championship series." Caroline reached into her backpack and pulled out a water bottle, taking a swig before continuing.

"The final game was a pitcher's duel, scoreless until the bottom of the sixth inning, when my team finally scraped across two runs. All I had to do was get three outs, and the title would be ours. The first two hitters hit easy pop-ups to the infield. I tried not to think about it as I faced the last hitter. I threw a drop ball and a change-up for called strikes. I threw a curve ball that the girl fouled off. I followed with a rise ball, which she swung at and missed. Strike three, ball game, we won."

"Why do I get the feeling that's not the happy ending?" Connor watched as Caroline reached down and took the last fry, popping it into her mouth.

Caroline nodded as she chewed, her eyes shining with moisture. "It was happy, for about a second. As everyone ran to me, jumping and screaming and celebrating, this stabbing pain shot through my elbow. My hand went weak, and my last two fingers went numb. I tried to celebrate, but the pain was too much. I got hauled off to the emergency room. Partially torn tendon, and cubital tunnel syndrome. I had surgery, but my softball career was over."

"Caroline, I'm so sorry. That's awful." Connor clenched his hand into a fist to keep from reaching for hers across the table.

"Don't be sorry. I don't need pity. It's just the way my life is, apparently." Caroline crossed her arms over her chest as she spoke.

"I didn't mean that I pity you. I just meant I'm sorry you had to go through that."

Caroline looked down at the table. "Thank you. But I'm still a part of the team. I get to be a manager."

"But that has to be hard on you." Connor tilted his head to the side as Caroline looked back up at him.

She studied him for a few seconds, her eyes full. "Yeah, it can be. But I'm makin' it work." She attempted to smile.

Connor was beginning to fill in the question marks he had regarding Caroline and why she was taking the weanling class. She'd lost her escape from horses and was, maybe, trying to find her way again. As he thought of the weanling class, he remembered something else he had wanted to ask her since their practical.

"I have another question, but I don't have any more food to give you for your answer." He gestured toward the empty fry box.

Caroline laughed. "That's alright. Go ahead."

"Yesterday, after Luna freaked out, you didn't give her to me, or take any time like Dr. Carnes suggested. You just calmed her down and went back to the cones and picked up where you left off. How come?"

Caroline's eyes dropped to the table. "Well, I'm sure by now you've figured out I'm a little nervous around her?"

Connor was shocked by her honesty. "Yeah, I have. But I wasn't going to say anything."

She looked up. "I appreciate that. More than you know." Her eyes held his and Connor could sense how sincere she was being. "Anyway, it was because of my fear. I knew if I gave Luna to you, that would be the end of it. I wouldn't ever take her back. Not to do the practical, not at any other time in the class. I would have been done. If I hadn't just kept going..."

Her eyes went up to the ceiling as her voice broke off. Connor saw her close them and swallow before bringing her gaze back to him. She didn't speak, but lifted both of her hands, palms up. Connor nodded, understanding.

I think you're amazing, he thought to himself, but bit his tongue to keep from speaking it. It wasn't the time, and there was still a lot he wanted to know. Like why she was taking the class at all. He hesitated, as he tried to figure out if this was the right moment.

Studying her, he realized she was looking past him. She smiled and waved at a group of guys as they walked by, but none of them acknowledged her. They were all focused on a tall blond guy who was gabbing away in the middle of their group. Connor watched her smile disappear as they passed. She stared down at the table, pulling at her fingers.

"Caroline? You okay?"

She only nodded her head in response.

"Did you know them?"

She looked up then. "Yeah. They're from the baseball team. The one in the middle, doing all the talking, his name is Ryan. He's my boyfriend."

Connor coughed, working to hide the surprise that hit him. "You, uh, never mentioned you had a boyfriend."

"That was one question you didn't ask." Caroline chuckled.

"Well, I guess that's true." Connor chuckled also. "So, a baseball player, huh? I guess that makes sense. Is he any good?"

"Yeah. He's one of the stars of the team. He hit for the cycle in their game over the weekend."

"That's a big deal, I'm guessing?"

"Oh yeah, pretty rare. He's been getting calls from major league scouts. He's excited. And obsessed."

Connor watched her face fall as she said the last part. "And what about you?"

"Me?" Her eyebrows crinkled in confusion.

"Are you as excited and obsessed as he is?" Connor grinned, trying to bring back the lightheartedness from earlier.

Caroline shrugged. "I'm happy for him, if that's what you mean."

"Kinda."

"It's all he talks about," Caroline sighed. "I try to be happy and supportive, but it can be a little much for me at times, considering." She glanced down at her right elbow.

"I can understand that."

Caroline nodded her head at his words. "So, do I get to ask you all sorts of questions now? Should I go get some fries, or tater tots, or something to use as an incentive for you to answer?" Caroline smirked at him.

"You can ask me whatever you want, but..." Connor paused to pull his phone out of his pocket, checking the time. "I have a class to get to. I'm guessing you probably do, too?"

Caroline peered over the table to read his phone. "Oh, yeah, I do. I didn't realize what time it had gotten to be."

They both stood, and Caroline put her textbook and headphones into her backpack. Connor strode over to the closest trash can, disposing of the trash from his food.

"Which way are you going?" Connor grabbed his backpack and swung it over his shoulders.

"That way." Caroline pointed.

"Me, too." They walked through the union, managing to stay together as they navigated the crowd.

"Can I ask one quick thing? As we walk?" Caroline glanced over at him.

"Sure."

"Do you have a girlfriend?" Caroline bit her lip to keep from grinning.

"Not at all what I thought you'd ask." Connor chuckled. "No, I don't have a girlfriend.

Caroline giggled. "Glad I could clear that up."

Connor laughed. He opened the door for Caroline, and she giggled again as she passed through. He smiled at the sound, glad that at least for the time being, she had forgotten about the boyfriend who hadn't noticed her waving at him.

Ten

THE PITCHING CIRCLE AND THE ENTIRE GAME looked different from the dugout than from the field. Sure, Caroline had spent plenty of innings behind the chain link, when her team was hitting, or if she wasn't pitching, but this felt more isolated. Like she was watching from a distance.

Which she was.

She was an outsider. She was no longer in a uniform, no longer a part of the buzz or the adrenaline. Her actions, her abilities, no longer had any effect on the outcome of the game. All she was doing was charting pitches. It was all she could do.

It was a reality that had become more and more clear ever since her talk with Connor.

What made watching and charting even harder was that the team was winning. Not just this game, but the whole tournament. Undefeated, they were now in the championship game.

Vanessa had hit a three-run homerun her last at bat, giving them a comfortable lead. They were headed to the top of the seventh inning, and Sarah was pitching a no-hitter. No one on the opposing team had been able to get a ball out of the infield.

"What did we throw this girl last time?" Coach Tara looked over Caroline's shoulder at the clipboard in her hand.

Caroline studied the chart. Her job was to mark down which pitches they called in which location, in what order, if it was a ball or a strike, and what the hitter did with the pitch. "Two drop balls outside, a curve outside, then a screwball coming in, which she popped up to shortstop."

"Thanks." Coach Tara signaled to the catcher what she wanted Sarah to throw. "Drop inside," she murmured to Caroline. She wrote it down and waited to see where it went.

Caroline watched as Sarah stepped on to the pitching rubber, took the signal from the catcher, and spun the ball in her glove, finding the right grip. Caroline imagined her fingers around the seams, and as Sarah threw the pitch, her muscles remembered how it felt: her wrist snapping by her hip, turning her hand over to get the right spin, to make the ball start in the strike zone, then spiral downward as it reached home plate. The batter swung, hitting a weak ground ball to Vanessa at third base. She fielded it and made a clean throw to first. One pitch, one out.

"Fastball in, then change up away." Caroline finished writing down the last out as she told Coach Tara what they had done earlier to get the next batter. "She grounded out to Sarah."

Coach Tara nodded her head. "Let's go with a curve ball, outside corner." She flashed the call to the catcher, her fingers moving through a set of numbers. Holding her breath, Caroline penciled it on to the paper and waited.

Again, as Sarah went through her delivery, Caroline imagined herself going through the motions. She stepped across her body with her left foot, just enough to give herself leverage to pull the pitch across from hip to hip, creating the spin that would cause the ball to dive away from the hitter.

"Strike!" The batter froze as the ump called the pitch. Caroline marked it down.

"Change up, in." Coach Tara smiled at her as she wrote it down.

Sarah nodded as the catcher gave her the call. Caroline closed her eyes, picturing her wrist staying stiff as she flipped her hand, taking about ten miles an hour of velocity off the ball. She heard the ting of the bat and looked out just in time to see Sarah fielding the ball. Two pitches, two outs.

"Alright, one more to go." Coach Tara glanced over at Caroline. "How'd we get her?"

Caroline looked down at her chart. "Drop in, change in, screw ball up and in, struck out."

Coach Tara went through a number of signs again, relaying to the catcher what she wanted thrown. The catcher turned and gave the pitch to Sarah, but before Coach Tara could tell Caroline what to mark down, Sarah shook her head no, calling off the pitch. The catcher gave another sign, and Sarah agreed.

"What'd she shake off?" Caroline clutched the side of the clipboard.

"Screw ball." Coach Tara pursed her lips together as she studied the field.

"And we have no idea what she's throwing?"

"Nope."

Caroline stared out toward the mound as the pitcher worked to get her grip. She saw the girl line up her middle finger on the seam, and curl her index finger, just a touch.

Rise ball, Caroline thought to herself, not daring to tell Coach Tara. A rise ball was a strikeout pitch, something you threw when you were ahead in the count. Very few pitchers ever threw it as the first pitch, unless they were sure they could start it low enough to get it called for a strike. And that was when you were pretty certain the hitter wasn't going to swing at it. Caroline wasn't sure Sarah was experienced enough to do that, to have that kind of knowledge.

Please throw it for a ball. Caroline tightened her right hand into a fist, clenching it so tight that her elbow and pinky finger ached. She held onto the pain, remembering how to throw the last pitch she had ever thrown. Keep your weight back, shoulders behind your hip. Have a long arm, knuckles reaching toward the ground. Lead with your pinky, snap the doorknob open.

Sarah fired away, and Caroline watched as the ball started to rise, but then flattened out into the heart of the strike zone. The hitter made contact. A hardline drive to center field.

"Get there." Coach Tara's whisper was the only noise in the dugout. All eyes were glued on their center fielder, April. She was sprinting across the grass, eyes glued to the ball. Caroline thought it was going to bounce, but April dove, stretching her entire body out. The ball smacked into her glove. Three outs. Ball game.

No hitter.

Caroline wrote down the pitch and where it went as everyone around her began celebrating. She slid the pencil into the clip at the top of the clipboard and handed it to Coach Tara.

"That was close." Coach Tara put the clipboard down into her backpack.

"Yeah. You may want to talk to her about using a rise ball as a first pitch." Caroline stood and stretched her arms out over her head.

"No kidding. But not today. I'll let her enjoy the

moment. We'll talk about it next practice."

Caroline nodded her head as she watched Sarah give April a huge hug, thanking her teammate for the catch she had made to end the game. Everyone was high-fiving, chattering in their excitement over the win.

But she was in the dugout.

She turned away and got to work, cleaning up and putting away any equipment that belonged to the team.

As she reached for the broom, she saw Coach Sullivan jog out to the outfield where the team was huddled, waiting for him to start the after-game talk. In his hand, he held the game ball.

Caroline waited, leaning on the broom handle, and watched him present the ball to Sarah. The pitcher beamed, holding the ball with both hands as everybody clapped. Tears sprung to Caroline's eyes, and she was grateful no one else was in the dugout to see.

What she would give to have that ball again. To be in control of the game, to dominate the other team. To have a purpose. To feel needed.

Caroline went back to sweeping, focusing on the clouds of dust she formed with each push of the bristles. She stared at the circling sand, letting it take her back to the first game ball she had received as a sophomore in high school.

"Let's go, Maya! You got this!" Caroline wrapped her fingers through the chain link fence of the dugout and cheered for her teammate in the batter's box. It was the bottom of the sixth inning of the state championship game. Neither team had scored yet, but they had a runner on second base, and one of their best hitters was up.

Caroline watched as the opposing pitcher delivered the ball, missing the strike zone for ball one. Maya stepped out of the box as the catcher threw the ball back to the circle, taking a couple of practice swings to stay prepared. She turned back to the plate and got ready for the next pitch.

The pitcher didn't want to throw another ball, so she came into the strike zone. Maya swung the bat, hitting a line drive to right field for a base hit. Caroline and her other teammates screamed and jumped up and down as Tina sprinted from second to third. Their cheers and cries grew even louder as she turned for home.

The right fielder collected the ball and threw it toward home plate. Tina and the ball arrived in a dead tie, but Tina slid around the catcher, avoiding the tag, reaching through the swirling dust from her slide to touch home plate. The entire team erupted out of the dugout to celebrate when the umpire called her safe.

They moved their celebration back to the dugout, so the next hitter could go. Maya had moved to second base on the throw to the plate, and with just one inning left to play, they could use any run they could score.

Caroline resumed her spot on the dugout fence, hoping they could get that second run in. She had been pitching a great game, but another run of support would take some pressure off her. And the pressure was on.

She was throwing a no-hitter.

No one had said it out loud, so they wouldn't jinx it, and she knew she shouldn't have it on her mind, but she did. She wanted it, and she was three outs away from accomplishing it.

The clank of the bat on the ball got her attention. She watched as the ball sailed toward left field, her fingers clenching the fence as the ball sailed deeper and deeper, begging it to go out. But the left fielder tracked it to the base of the wall where she made the catch. Caroline sighed.

She would have to finish this with only one run on the board.

She took a minute, gathering her glove and pulling her ponytail back through her hat. She closed her eyes, refocusing on what she needed to do. A no-hitter or not, she needed to go win this game, the state championship. She had to throw strikes, to get outs. And that's just what she planned on doing.

Caroline jogged out to the circle. Picking up the ball, she snapped it into her glove a couple of times, loosening her finger and her wrist. She lined her feet up and went through her warm-up pitches, the ball spinning away from her with ease. She was ready to go.

Placing her feet on the rubber, she looked down to the catcher forty-three feet away. She took her sign: screw ball. She went through the pitch in her mind, thinking of how to throw it. She fired, getting the batter to hit a dinky ground ball to the shortstop for the first out.

Two to go. Caroline got the ball back from her first baseman and walked to the back of the circle, taking a deep breath. She bent down and got a handful of dirt, rubbing it over her palm to help her grip the ball. Her throwing hand felt damp in anticipation as she wiped it on her pants, then stepped back up to the rubber.

Drop ball. She thought about the spin before she began her delivery. She wound and snapped, inducing another ground ball for the second out.

Caroline could feel the crowd's anticipation. She could sense the energy pulsing through her team. Everyone knew this was it, the last batter she would have to face if she could get the out. The championship would be theirs.

The no-hitter would be hers.

She forced another deep breath as she stepped to the rubber to get her sign. Another drop ball. She repeated the motion and spin she had just thrown for a called strike one. She got the ball back, replanted her feet on the rubber, and waited for the next call.

Caroline nodded her head, agreeing to the changeup. *Keep your arm speed up*, she reminded herself as she worked the ball in her glove to get the grip she wanted. She flipped her wrist as she released, slowing down the pitch for a called strike two.

The fans for their team stood up in the stands, recognizing they needed just one more strike to win. Caroline took the ball to the edge of the pitching circle, looking out at the center field fence, then up to the lights shining down on the field. The last beams of light from the sunset glowed over the top of the mountains. The May breeze ruffled the end of her ponytail. She closed her eyes. *You can do this. Throw a strike. It's that easy.*

Turning back, determination echoing in each step, she took to the rubber. The catcher relayed the sign to her. Screw ball, up and in.

With two strikes on the hitter, Caroline knew she needed to make this a chase pitch, something out of the strike zone that would trick the batter into swinging and missing. She pictured where she wanted it to go, and off she went.

She gave the pitch a little extra oomph, grunting as she snapped the ball. It ran in and up, going right where she wanted it. The batter swung through it, missing by several inches. Strike three. Three outs. Ballgame.

State championship.

No-hitter.

Caroline threw her glove up in the air as her teammates invaded the pitching circle, throwing their arms around each other, sweat and tears mixing as they screamed in celebration. Their coach ran out to join them, stopping first to get the ball from the umpire. He pushed his way to the middle of their huddle to find Caroline.

"Great game, girls! Let's keep celebrating! But first, Caroline, here's your game ball!"

Everyone cheered her name as she accepted the ball, taking it in both hands, a large smile stretching across her entire face.

"Caroline?" Coach Sullivan put a hand on her shoulder, stopping her from sweeping.

Caroline spun around. "Yeah?"

"I think the dugout is all clean now, if you want to quit."

Her eyes snapped up and looked around. Everyone was gone except for the two of them.

"Oh. I guess I lost track of time." She sat the broom back in the corner, behind the bench.

"You seemed like you were lost in thought. Anything you want to talk about?"

Caroline hesitated. Watching the tournament, seeing Sarah's no-hitter, then going back to her no-hitter as a sophomore in high school had brought her to a startling conclusion. She had started softball to escape the pity her friends and family felt for her because of her accident. She had focused on pitching to help her heart move on from the pain of losing Beau. She had started something new, but only after letting something go.

Blinking, she realized she had to move on. Again.

"Actually, yeah, there is."

"What's up?"

"You remember how a few weeks ago, after you saw me trying to pitch again, you told me that eventually something would make sense again?" She stared down at her tennis shoes as she spoke.

"Yes, I do. Do you think you've got it already?"

"No, not even close. But I think my first step in finding what makes sense is leaving all of this behind."

Coach Sullivan studied her, taking his time developing a response. "I'm guessing today was kind of hard for you."

Caroline nodded her head in agreement. "Not just today. The whole weekend. And every practice leading up to it."

"I can understand that. So, you're saying you quit?" A small smile lifted the corners of the coach's mouth.

Caroline gave a short laugh. "Yeah, I guess that is what I'm saying."

Coach Sullivan came closer and gave her left shoulder a squeeze. "Alright, kiddo. If you decide you want to come back, please don't hesitate. You'll always have a spot here."

"Thank you, Coach. Thank you for this opportunity, and I don't just mean as a manager." Caroline's voice wavered as tears closed in on her throat.

"You're very welcome. Keep in touch, alright?" He smiled and winked at her.

"I will." Caroline collected her bag and water bottle from the bench and climbed up the steps onto the field. She paused, taking everything in one last time. The way the grass was the perfect shade of green. The snow-white chalk that drew the batters' boxes and the pitching circle. The red clay dirt that had stained hundreds of pairs of her socks throughout the years. The bullpen.

Her eyes settled on the crates of balls, and she remembered the weight of the ball in her hand. The burn of the seam over her fingers as she spun each pitch with precision. The slide of her back foot as she dragged it behind her. The snap of the ball in the catcher's mitt as the batter swung and missed.

She tore herself away and walked down the narrow, one-way street that took her to the mall. Ducking her head, one tear slid down her cheek as she jogged toward the setting sun, working to avoid eye contact with anyone she met. The purple and navy shades of dusk settled in around her as she found her car. Her keys slipped through her fingers and clattered to the concrete. Bending over, she collected the keys, and herself, before opening her door and sitting down. She made eye contact with the reflection in the review mirror. Her blue eyes were clouded with unshed tears and sadness, and a small ache had settled in around her heart. The pain didn't surprise her, as she thought about her decision to quit the team. As she recognized the life she had just left behind.

What shocked her was the small sense of relief.

Eleven

THE LIGHT-BLUE OCTOBER SKY WAS DOTTED with soft white clouds that shaded the sun every few minutes. Connor sat on the top of the pipe fence, watching as Caroline worked with Luna, teaching her to walk over a small bridge. All of the babies had been doing well with leading, so the class had graduated from the grass pasture to the dry lot next to the barn. An obstacle course was set up there, and the weanlings were learning how to cross the bridge, step over poles on the ground, walk onto a tarp, and back through a set of poles shaped like an L.

Connor was enjoying the weather and the new challenge the obstacles presented for the babies, but he was struggling to shake off his irritation. They were being watched. Not the class, but just Caroline and him.

By Caroline's boyfriend.

Connor was sure Caroline hadn't invited him, as Ryan stood away from the barn, careful to keep his distance. He was leaning against one of the buildings used as classrooms for agricultural classes taught at the farm. His arms were folded across his chest, and Connor could feel his eyes burning a hole into the back of his neck. If Caroline knew he was there, she hid it well.

"Good girl, Luna." Connor watched as Caroline praised the filly for putting one foot up on the bridge. She rubbed her neck, then turned her away, rewarding her for her effort. She beamed over at Connor. "She's doing so well."

"Yeah, she's doing great." *And she's not the only one,* Connor added to himself. In the two weeks since their practical and the plastic bag incident, Caroline had become much more relaxed. She still got nervous and scared, and there were times when she still handed Luna over to him when she felt overwhelmed, but it was happening less often, and she was recovering quicker. He wasn't sure what had brought on the change, but she seemed happier overall.

After their conversation in the union, Connor had gone home and Googled her name, wanting to know more about her softball career. He had found dozens of articles written about her and learned that she had won state championships her sophomore, junior, and senior years of high school. It was obvious she had worked hard to excel at the sport, chasing after success like her life depended on it.

And Connor thought maybe it had.

It made sense to him, why she had needed something else to focus on, to obsess over, after her accident. Being around horses must have been too hard for her, so she moved on the only way she could figure out how.

By finding something else, someone else, she could be.

Caroline had Luna back at the bridge, working again to get the filly to put her feet on it. As he watched, Connor caught glimpses of the girl he had watched from a distance years ago, the one who was fearless, the one who belonged on a horse. He hadn't seen that girl in any of the softball pictures he had found.

Connor didn't recognize the softball version of Caroline. Sure, he could tell it was her, but her eyes were different, like she was searching for something. She looked too focused, too harsh, almost cold, as if her purpose in life was to dominate the batter in the box before her. The contrast between that Caroline and the Caroline in front of him was startling.

Connor glanced over his shoulder to see if Ryan was still there. He didn't look for long, as he didn't want to make eye contact with the guy. The angry look on his face unsettled him.

Connor blinked as he began to realize why Ryan was watching. If Connor didn't recognize Caroline in her softball pictures, Ryan wouldn't recognize the girl who was working with the horse. He wondered if Ryan had noticed the change in Caroline in the past two weeks, too, and was trying to make sense of it.

"Thatta girl, Luna. One more step." Connor turned his attention back to Caroline. The same front foot Luna had placed on the bridge before was on it again, and Caroline was coaxing her to step up with her other front leg. The filly was pulling against the pressure Caroline had on her lead but wasn't fighting her. Caroline stayed patient, waiting for even the slightest forward movement.

Luna sighed and picked up her foot. Caroline pushed her hand forward, releasing the hold she had on the rope. Luna put her second foot down on the bridge.

"Good girl." Caroline's fingers circled the white marking on the filly's head. She let her stand there for a moment before backing her away, and leading her toward Connor.

Connor hopped off the fence as they approached. "That was awesome."

"Yeah, it was. She's so brave." Caroline lifted her hand for a high five. Connor reached up and clapped his hand against hers, cringing on the inside at the thought of Ryan's eyes still focused on them.

Caroline looked at her wrist to check the time on her Fitbit. "I know there's still a few minutes left, but what do you think about letting her be done for the day?"

"I think that's a good idea. Getting that second foot up on the bridge seems like a pretty good place to stop." Connor scratched Luna on her shoulder. The filly leaned into his touch as he found an itchy spot. "You still free to work on our midterm project tomorrow?"

"Yeah, around 1:00?"

"That'll work." Connor gave her a reassuring smile. "You found directions okay?"

"Yep. I-Ten to Highway Eighty-Three. Twenty-five miles, then turn right, go another two miles then another right. Then follow the dirt road all the way to the driveway, right?"

He smiled again, impressed that she had memorized the instructions from the GPS. "You got it."

"Alright, everyone, that's all the time we have for today. Let's take them back to their field," Dr. Carnes interrupted. "Have a good weekend."

Caroline looked up at Connor. "Do you mind taking her out? I need to get to my next class a few minutes early today."

"Sure thing." Connor took the lead rope from her, snapping his eyes to where Ryan had been standing. To his relief, he was gone. He was thankful he hadn't stuck around to bother Caroline.

"Thanks, I'll see you tomorrow." Connor watched as Caroline squeezed out of the gate ahead of the horses, ducking into the tack room door and the classroom beyond to collect her things. Connor turned his head as Luna pulled on his arm, straining to follow her friends as they headed to the pasture. "Alright, little girl. Let's go."

Connor listened as everyone around him chattered away about their weekend plans. His mind drifted to their midterm project, a presentation on a well-known trainer and their methods. He and Caroline had chosen Pat Parelli, and they had started their research earlier in the week.

Leading their young horses, the students arrived at the field and worked together to release the horses at the same time. Rebel squealed as his halter slid down off his face, breaking into a gallop as he headed to the far end of the pasture. Luna caught up to him with ease, the only other baby that could run that fast. Connor chuckled as she nipped at Rebel's neck as they turned the corner, enjoying their competitiveness.

He latched the gate after the last student went through and walked into the barn to get his stuff. As he swung his backpack over his shoulder, Dr. Carnes walked into the room.

"Connor, I've been wanting to tell you how good of a job you're doing. Not just with Luna, but with Caroline as well. It seems you've really been able to help her out."

"Thank you, sir." Connor smiled back at the professor. "I've been enjoying every minute of class."

"Good to hear. I'll see you on Monday."

Connor walked to his truck, his eyes down as he thought about Caroline. Dr. Carnes seemed to think Connor was the reason Caroline was doing so well, but he wasn't so sure. He had done his best to help her whenever she needed him, and to be her friend, but he couldn't think of anything specific he had done that would have caused the relaxation and confidence he had seen in her since the practical.

"Hey!" A voice yelled at him as he opened the door to his truck. Connor froze as he saw Ryan jogging toward him from a car parked across the lot. *He didn't leave...*

Slowing down to walk as he reached the tailgate, Ryan's eyebrows were creased, and his green eyes reflected tension.

"Who are you?" Ryan spit out.

"Connor Taylor." He held out his hand to shake Ryan's.

Ryan eyed Connor's extended hand then ignored it, crossing his arms instead. Connor let his hand fall back down to his side.

"What do you want with my girlfriend?"

Hesitating, Connor prayed. *Lord, give me the right words here. Help me calm him down.* He cleared his throat. "I'm her partner in class, that's all. We were assigned to work together."

Ryan glared at him through squinted eyes. "I don't buy it. There's something more going on here."

"Why do you say that?"

"One, I saw how you watched her in class just now. I'm not an idiot, I can see you like her. Two, she's changed since working with you. She quit her manager position with the softball team, and she wants nothing to do with it, or baseball, anymore."

"She quit? When?"

"A couple weeks ago."

Nodding his head, Connor felt a cool sense of realization working its way through him. The timeline matched when Caroline had started acting lighter, happier.

"Don't play dumb with me. I'm sure it's you who convinced her," Ryan snapped, annoyed by Connor's silence.

"Nope, wasn't me. I didn't even know she quit until just now. She didn't say a word to me."

"I don't believe you. I want you to stay away from her."

Dropping his arms to his sides, Ryan clenched his fists.

Connor pressed his lips together and swallowed. "I can't do that. Like I said, I'm her partner in class."

"Then ask for a different partner."

"I won't do that."

Ryan stepped closer. "And why not?"

Connor gulped, studying the guy in front of him. His anger was easy to see, but underneath, Connor thought he was afraid. "Ryan, did she tell you why she's taking this class?"

Confusion clouded Ryan's expression. "She needs a major and didn't know what to pick. Why?"

"So, you don't know why she picked this?"

"She didn't pick this." Losing his patience, Ryan ground his teeth together. "Her advisor picked it for her. Something about it being a good fit. Again, why?"

"A good fit?"

"Yeah, 'cause her mom does this horse thing, I don't know, so her advisor thought she should too."

Horse thing. This guy pays attention, Connor scoffed to himself. "Just her mom? Not her? She's never done the horse thing?" He had to bite his lip to keep from smiling at his use of Ryan's words.

"Not until this stupid class. She played softball instead." Ryan tipped his head. "Stop asking me questions. I'm the one questioning you here."

"Sorry. What else did you want to ask?"

Pausing, Ryan glared at Connor. "I guess that's it. Stay away from her, got it?"

Connor shrugged. "I'm not gonna do that. She has a gift, Ryan. I'm just trying to help her."

Rolling his eyes, Ryan cleared his throat. "Listen. She doesn't need you. Or your help. Or her gift." He lifted his hands and put air quotation marks around the word gift. "She has me. That's all she needs." Ryan turned and headed for his car.

Sighing, Connor opened the door to his truck. "You don't even notice her," he muttered as he shoved his backpack into the cab.

"Excuse me?" Ryan turned back toward Connor.

"Nothing, just forget it."

Ryan closed the gap between them in four long strides. He stopped just short of where Connor was standing. "You better start talking."

"You don't see her or care enough to know who she is. The other day, you walked right by her in the union. She smiled and waved and was happy to see you, and you blew right by her. Too busy with that little entourage of yours." Connor felt his own anger burning, and took a breath to try to rein it in.

"How do you know anything about that?" Ryan hissed.

"I was sitting with her when it happened."

"You hung out with my girlfriend?" Heat and blood rose to Ryan's face, turning his cheeks crimson red.

"No, not really. It was raining and there weren't any other open seats. I ran into her coincidentally and asked if I could sit down. She told me I could."

Tightening his jaw, Ryan took a step closer. "You're pretty dang lucky I'm here on a baseball scholarship and am close to getting drafted. That's the only thing keeping me from knocking you out right now."

Every muscle in Connor's body stiffened at the threat. He opened his mouth to tell Ryan to leave.

"Connor, is everything okay?" Dr. Carnes interrupted, calling from near his car.

Clearing his throat, Connor took a step back. "Yes, sir.

Ryan here was just leaving."

"This isn't over," Ryan snarled low enough just for Connor to hear.

"But it is. Go, before you lose your precious scholarship." Connor pointed toward Ryan's car.

Straightening at his words, Ryan pasted an annoyed half smile on his lips. Connor watched as he jogged to his car, got in, and sped away. He looked toward Dr. Carnes, who was staring at him. When Ryan's car was out of sight, Dr. Carnes lifted his hand toward Connor, before driving away himself.

Connor climbed into his truck and cranked the engine. Breathing in and out, he closed his eyes. *Lord, I'm sorry I got so angry. Thank You for controlling that situation and not letting it get out of hand. Please, if Ryan sees Caroline tonight, take care of her. I can't stand the thought of him hurting her.*

Connor reached for his auxiliary cord and dug his phone out of his pocket to plug it in. He called up his driving playlist as he prepared for the hour or so drive home. He tapped the shuffle button, and "Run" by Urban Rescue sprang to life in the speakers.

Letting the lyrics fall over him, he put his truck in reverse and left the parking lot. He whispered along as the first verse continued. "Please don't leave me where I am. Take me back where love began. Though my eyes can't see the end, I believe You have a plan."

Connor turned onto the road and headed for the interstate. He let the song work its way into his heart as he drove and pictured Caroline. There was a plan; he just had to wait it out and keep praying for her every step of the way.

Twelve

CONNOR WAS ANXIOUS ALL MORNING as he helped with chores around the ranch. He was pulling his phone out every few minutes, checking the time and looking for any calls or text messages, while he helped feed the horses and clean their stalls. Now he was sitting down to eat lunch with his parents and couldn't sit still.

He bit off a chunk of his BLT sandwich and chewed, tapping his foot on the leg of the table. Again, he pressed the home button of his phone to check the time. 12:42.

"Connor, please. You're driving me nuts." His mom reached over and put her hand on his knee, a kind smile on her face. He stopped his bouncing foot and smiled back.

Connor swallowed. "Sorry, guess I'm kind of restless."

His dad snorted. "That's an understatement. You've been like this all morning."

"Must be some midterm project to get you this stirred up." Jessica winked at him.

"Some project indeed." Greg laughed, setting his sandwich down on his plate.

"Alright, guys. Give me a break. Just remember what we talked about. Don't say anything about knowing her parents. Or her."

"We got it, we got it. You only told us a hundred times." This time, his dad winked at him, still teasing.

"Oh yeah, our lips are sealed." His mom pushed her lips together, turning an invisible key and throwing it over her shoulder.

Connor rolled his eyes and shook his head as he took another bite. "You guys are impossible."

Outside, Connor heard tires on the gravel driveway. He peered out the window, recognizing Caroline's little blue Nissan. He hurried back to the table, popping the last bit of his sandwich into his mouth. He took his plate to the kitchen as he chewed, turning on the water as it crashed from his hands into the sink. He heard his parents' laughter from the table.

"Sorry!" he called out over the running water. "If nothing else, at least I'm providing you guys with some entertainment."

Connor finished rinsing his dish and headed to the entryway to pull on his boots. He yanked the legs of his jeans down over the shafts and turned for the door.

As the screen door banged shut behind him, he saw Caroline bending over near her car petting their two Australian Shepherds and Golden Retriever. Their tails were wagging, and they were licking her face.

"They sure are lousy guard dogs, but they make a great welcoming committee." Connor jogged down the porch steps and walked toward them.

"They're very sweet." Caroline stood up and pulled her blond braid over her shoulder. "What are their names?"

"Yeah, they're sweet, and spoiled rotten. The Golden is Allie. The red one is Ace, and this one here is Blue, since he has blue eyes." Connor knelt down and scratched Blue behind the ears.

"Blue 'cause he has blue eyes? That's quite original of you." Caroline grinned down at him.

"Hey now, I was seven. This guy has been my buddy for a long time."

"Aww, alright. No more grief over his name."

"Thank you." Connor straightened and looked out across the parking lot to the barns. "I thought maybe we'd start with a tour before we get to work? I could show you the barns and some of the horses."

He watched as Caroline's gaze followed his down to the barns. Her smile started to fall from her lips, but she recovered before she answered. "Sure, sounds good."

As they walked side by side to the first large barn, Connor glanced at her from the side, searching for any signs indicating Ryan had told her about what had happened yesterday, or that he had taken his anger out on her. But Caroline seemed fine, a little tense, but that was normal, considering they were about to walk into a barn full of horses.

"What?" Caroline turned her head and caught him looking at her.

He looked toward the barn, thinking of what to say. "So, uh, how was your Friday night?"

"Pretty quiet. I just stayed home and studied. What about you?"

Connor worked to keep the shock off his face. "The same, actually. You didn't do anything with Ryan?"

"No, he had a late practice."

Connor nodded his head as they entered the first barn. "Anyway, this is where the broodmares and babies live."

Caroline's eyes widened as she stepped inside the door. Her eyes looked over everything. Connor tried to see it for the first time through her eyes.

The barn was immaculate. The aisle was lined with spotless black rubber mats. Each stall had a halter and lead rope hanging next to the door, in identical placement. Every horse had a net full of hay and sparkling water buckets.

"Wow." Caroline interrupted the silence. "This is incredible."

"Thank you. I'm lucky to call this home." Connor walked to the first stall, answering the soft nicker that called out to him. He reached out and scratched the mare behind her ears.

Caroline followed him and read her nameplate out loud. "Power of a Dream. That's pretty."

"Pretty just like her." Connor agreed. "We call her Dream. She was my sister's jumper."

"Is that the ranch's focus? Jumpers?"

"And eventers." Connor watched for any kind of reaction from her as he said the word. "Really all sport horses, including some Thoroughbred racers. We occasionally do other types, if a client has a specific request."

"That's awesome." Caroline kept her eyes on Dream, taking in her sweet face and kind eye. She took a step toward her and lifted her hand.

"She's a love bug. She won't hurt you."

Caroline nodded as she let the mare smell her. She reached up and scratched her the same way Connor had, smiling as the mare leaned into her touch.

"See, I told you she's a love bug." Connor fought off the memories that tried to swirl to the surface as he watched Dream with Caroline. The scene was one he'd seen play out a million times between his sister and her horse.

"Yeah, she is. I'm guessing she's retired now? Since she's in the broodmare barn?"

"You got it. She's in foal with her first baby."

"How high did she jump?"

"She was competing at three feet, six inches to three feet, nine inches, but they were jumping about four feet in practice. She had the talent and heart for more, but uh, plans changed, I guess you could say."

Caroline turned to face him as she heard the change in his voice, but she kept one hand on Dream's cheek. She studied him for a minute before a small smile crossed her lips. "I can understand that."

Yeah, I know you can, he thought to himself. He gave Dream one last pat, letting his hand run down her white blaze. "You ready to continue?"

"Sure. Bye, Dream." Caroline followed him down the rest of the barn aisle.

Every few stalls, he would stop to tell her something about each mare or weanling they passed. He noticed that her interest seemed genuine, as she walked up and greeted a few of the horses.

"This is the training and boarding barn," Connor told her when they walked into the second barn. It mirrored the first barn in style and size, but there were three tack rooms, one at each end and one in the middle. There were also wash racks and cross ties throughout, giving clients a place to wash, groom, and saddle their horses.

"You guys do training and boarding, too?" Again, Caroline's eyes swept the aisle, taking it all in.

"We don't do the training part. Two trainers run their businesses out of our facility, one for eventing and one for dressage." Connor saw her stiffen a little this time when he mentioned eventing. "My mom manages the boarders."

"Did your parents start this place?"

"No, actually my grandfather did, my dad's dad. My dad

took over after he graduated from college and married my mom."

"So, it's a family tradition." Caroline peeked into the large tack room near the entrance. "Is that your plan then, too? To run it when you're done with school?"

"Pretty much. I just love this place, and what we do here. Even if it wasn't in the family, I think I'd find something like this to do with my life."

"I think you would, too." Caroline smiled at him. "Can I ask what your favorite part is?"

"Of course." Connor began leading her down the aisle. "The breeding part is. I enjoy looking at pedigrees and analyzing competition results, whether that be dressage scores or racing times, or jump penalties. I look for patterns. Like, does a certain pedigree line have a knack for knocking rails, or going clear? Does a specific stallion throw babies that are always in the top three after dressage? When I find those patterns, I then try to see what they've been crossed with, and what works and what didn't work. If that makes any sense at all."

Caroline didn't say anything, causing Connor to look up at her. She was staring at him, but Connor couldn't read the expression on her face.

He stopped in front of the stall they were passing. "I'm sorry if that was more information than you were looking for."

Caroline laughed. "No, don't be sorry. I can see you're passionate about it and you don't need to be sorry for that. I'm impressed, that's all. And maybe a little jealous."

Connor tried not to blush from her compliment, focusing instead on the last part of her statement. "Nothing to be impressed over. Can I ask why you're jealous?"

Caroline looked straight into his eyes, and Connor

could sense how serious she had become. "Just that you seem to have life all figured out, I guess. You kinda sound like someone who's being doing this for years, not just starting."

Connor chuckled. "Nah, I don't have it all figured out. If you think I sound smart, you should hear my dad go on about it. He's way better than I am." Connor started walking again. "You ready to see the stallions?"

"Sure." Caroline fell into step beside him. "I bet you're not as far off from your dad as you think. Even if you are, I have no doubt you'll catch up."

Again, Connor had to work to keep the heat out of his cheeks. "Thank you."

"You're welcome."

They walked in silence to the smallest barn on the property. It had fewer stalls than the other barns, but they were bigger, and each one had an outdoor area attached to it, giving the stallions the option of being inside or out. The sweet smell of alfalfa filled the air as the stallions munched on it.

"How many stallions do you guys have?" Caroline twisted the end of her braid in her fingers as they stepped in.

"Four, or I guess I should say five. My dad just left to pick up a new one after lunch. We own three of them, including the new one. The other two we stand for their owners."

They came to a stop in front of the first stall. A light gray head hung over the door with his ears perked. Connor walked up to pet the stallion, but Caroline stayed back.

"Just Jasper," Caroline read the nameplate. "That's cute. What's his story?"

"He's a Thoroughbred, off the track. He ran pretty well

locally, won a few out-of-state, too. His babies haven't done much on the track but are proving to be good jumpers. We're mostly advertising him for sport horses now." He glanced at her over his shoulder. "You can come closer. He won't hurt you."

"I'm okay here. He's gorgeous."

"Yeah, he is." Connor studied her and could see in her eyes that she wanted to get closer. "I promise he won't do anything. He's as sweet as they come."

She paused for a moment before nodding her head and creeping closer. She lifted her fingers for the stallion to smell, staying close to Connor as she did. Jasper breathed into her hand, then licked her palm. Caroline giggled under her breath, reaching up to stroke his face.

"What about the other three?" Caroline leaned her shoulder against Jasper's door and ran her fingers through his forelock.

"There's Magician, a Hanoverian." Connor pointed toward a blood bay resting in the corner of his stall across the aisle. "He does dressage and still actively competes at third level."

"He looks amazing, really fit."

"You should see him go under saddle." Connor's eyes moved down the aisle. "Over there we have Still Around, a Swedish Warmblood. We call him Comic. He evented through preliminary, then suffered a tendon injury. He could probably still compete at the lower levels, but he's a half-brother to a horse who won a couple of five stars, the highest level there is, so the owner decided to breed him instead."

As Connor talked about him, Comic appeared over the door. He bobbed his head up and down and flopped his lips together, making a noise that sounded almost like applause. "I think I see why you call him Comic." Caroline laughed.

"Oh, yeah. He does all kinds of little tricks like that." Connor looked at the last stallion in the barn, the one next to Jasper. "And then we have Red Oak, or Oakley, as we refer to him. He's a Thoroughbred, but never raced. He's a retired Grand Prix jumper."

"They're all so impressive, Connor. I don't know how anyone could ever pick which one to breed their mare to. Or how you guys decide which ones to breed your mares to." Caroline was still petting Jasper, scratching a spot high up on his neck. The stallion's eyes were closed, enjoying the attention.

Connor laughed. "Like I said, it's about analyzing pedigrees and results, and looking for the patterns. It's as simple as that."

"Yeah, sounds simple enough." Caroline rolled her eyes.

"Anyway, we should probably head to the house and get started."

"Good point. Alright, Jasper, you be a good boy." Caroline gave the horse one last pat. Connor's boots clicked down the aisle as Caroline followed him out of the barn and to the house. Walking in silence, Connor noticed as Caroline looked back several times at the barns and the pastures.

As they started to walk up the porch steps, Connor heard the rattling sound of horse trailer tires. He turned to see the farm's small trailer spiraling down the curves of the driveway, his dad behind the wheel. Parking in front of the stallion barn, he climbed out of the truck and met another man who walked out of the barn. Caroline followed Connor's eyes.

"That's my dad and our stallion manager," Connor informed her.

"So that's the new stallion you said was coming?" Caroline watched as they opened the trailer door. Two pricked ears could be seen in the shadows. A tail swished back and forth as hooves stomped and pawed the floor.

"Yeah. He's a Thoroughbred. He was actually born here, but we sold him a couple years ago. The people who bought him sold him again, and he ended up in the wrong hands. He's now been neglected and abused. The rescue that picked him up found our information on his registration papers and asked if we'd take him back."

"That's so sad. But great that you guys were able to get him back." Their assignment forgotten, Caroline and Connor watched the horse back out of the trailer. "What's his name?"

"He's registered under The Lighthouse, barn name Edison."

Neither of them moved toward the house as they admired the horse. Even though his ribs and hip bones stuck out, Edison was gorgeous. A blond mane and tail stood out against his rich red coat. His athletic ability was easy to see as he walked, a light spring in each step. As Connor's dad tried to walk him into the barn, the horse leapt up, trying to pull away. He reared, pawing at the air.

"Whoa. It might take a while for him to trust us." Connor heard Caroline gasp as the stallion landed and kicked out with his hind legs as soon as his front feet touched the ground. Connor's dad was careful to keep ahold of him. "Poor guy. I can't imagine what he's been through to act like this."

Caroline didn't answer. Connor tore his gaze away from Edison to check on her. Her eyes were frozen on the scene in front of her as the men somehow got the stallion into the barn. Her face looked as white as chalk, and her arms were folded across her stomach.

"Caroline? Are you okay?" Connor watched as she tried to swallow but ended up coughing and choking instead. He took a step toward her, but she held up her hand.

When she could speak, she looked at him. "I'm okay. Just swallowed wrong."

Connor knew that was a lie, but as he studied the sweat beads on her forehead, he decided to let it go. "Alright, well, let's get to work then."

Inside the house, Connor lead Caroline toward the island in the kitchen where he had set his laptop. "I thought we could work here." He pulled out one of the stools, inviting her to sit. "Do you want anything to drink?"

"Water would be great. Thank you." Caroline pulled herself up onto the stool.

Connor reached into the cabinet and pulled out two tall glasses that were etched with a floral pattern. After filling them with ice and water from the dispenser on the shiny black fridge, he sat them down and circled around behind her to sit on the stool next to her. Opening his laptop, he typed in his password and called up the PowerPoint app so they could start formatting their slides.

They worked together well and had many of the same ideas when it came to slide design and how to present the information. Caroline smiled and laughed as they worked, relaxing more with each minute that passed. Finishing the PowerPoint, they scripted out what they would each say.

"Got any plans for the rest of the weekend?" Connor closed his laptop as Caroline stood and stretched.

"No, not really. Just more studying and homework. Chemistry takes more effort than anything else."

"Oh, yeah. It did for me, too. I bet it helps now that you have more time, since you quit your manager job with the softball team." The words were out before Connor could stop them. He pressed his lips closed and didn't look at her.

"How'd you find out about that?"

"I, uh...just heard about it. That's all." Connor looked at her, shrugging his shoulders.

"You're kinda bad at lying." A small smile found her lips. "You can tell me. It'll be okay."

"I don't know about that."

"Don't know about what?"

"That it'll be okay."

"It will be."

He hesitated, but the look on her face and the tone of her voice made him believe her. "Ryan told me."

"Ryan?" Confusion settled into her expression. "When did you talk to him?"

"Yesterday. He watched us during class, then came up to me in the parking lot when I was leaving."

"Ryan was at the farm?" Caroline's confusion turned to shock.

"Yeah, he was there."

"You didn't say anything to me during class about him being there." Caroline's eyes searched his. Connor wasn't sure what she found there, or how to reply. She looked down and shook her head. "What did he say to you?"

"Nothing too important."

"Connor." Caroline looked back up at him, her eyes firm.

"Maybe you should talk to Ryan."

"Connor. Please. Just tell me."

Connor couldn't handle the begging in her eyes. He exhaled through his mouth, the air whooshing from his lips. "Alright. He asked me what was going on between you and me. I told him we were just partners for class, but he didn't buy it. He said you've changed, and that he knows it's my fault, and that if it weren't for his baseball scholarship, he would have knocked me out."

Caroline's mouth fell open and all the color drained out of her cheeks. She gripped the back of the stool, her knuckles turning white. Connor didn't know Ryan, but from Caroline's reaction, he could tell the information he had given her didn't match the boy she knew in her heart.

Thirteen

CAROLINE FELT THE BLOOD COMING BACK into her cheeks as she managed to take a deep breath. Straightening and releasing her grip on the stool, she worked her fingers to get rid of the pain the tension had caused in her elbow.

"I shouldn't have told you." Connor's voice was full of concern, just louder than a whisper.

"No, I'm glad you did. I don't know what got into him." Caroline shrugged her shoulders. "I'm sorry he threatened you."

"Don't worry about it. I can take it." Connor puffed out his chest, a goofy grin on his kind face. Caroline felt relief as she saw the light come back into his brown eyes.

"Maybe, but you shouldn't have to."

"Caroline, it's not your fault."

But maybe it is, she said inside her head. Ryan had been shocked when she quit her manager position. He had accused her of changing, and she had denied it. She told him she was just trying to adjust, and that it hurt too much to be around softball every day. Somehow, he had turned it around and thought Connor was to blame. Just another example of how he didn't understand where she was at in her life.

She blinked, clearing her thoughts, and reached for her keys on the counter. "I should get going."

Connor nodded his head. "Are you going home? Or to talk to him?"

"I think I have to talk to him."

"Just be careful, okay?"

Caroline could see his worry as his forehead crinkled under his neat, but wavy bangs. "What do you mean?"

"He got pretty angry. I don't want you to get hurt."

Caroline was touched that he cared so much. "I won't."

Connor's eyes held hers. "Good. Come on, I'll walk you to your car."

He held the door open for her as they stepped onto the porch. Allie, Ace, and Blue jumped up from their beds to greet her again. She paused to give each of them a quick pat on the head before following Connor down the steps.

"I'll email you the PowerPoint and script, so you can go through it again before Monday." Connor shoved his hands into his pockets as she opened her door.

"That would be great. Thank you."

"No problem. I'll see you then." Connor took a few steps backward, toward the house.

"Enjoy the rest of the weekend." Ducking her head, she climbed into the driver's seat.

"Caroline?" Connor called out before she could shut the door.

"Yeah?"

"I'll be praying for you."

"If you think it'll help."

A slow smile spread across his face. "It will. It always helps." He lifted his hand in a wave as he turned and walked to the house.

Caroline shut the car door, hesitating before she started the engine. She rolled down the driveway, taking her time to absorb everything she had heard in the last few minutes.

She couldn't believe Ryan would do something like that. It went against everything she knew about him. Sure, he could be a little obsessive with baseball, and a little out of touch with her and what she was feeling, but he would never threaten to hurt somebody. Not ever.

But even through her surprise and disbelief, she knew Connor wasn't lying. He wouldn't make up something like this.

A few tears stung her eyes, but she was determined not to let them fall. The small, two-lane highway she had to take to get to the interstate stressed her out, and she didn't want to be crying as she drove through the curves. She tried to focus on the scenery instead. It was beautiful, with yellow grass covering the hills that rolled in every direction. Several ranches were spread out along the road, cows and horses dotting their fields. Peaceful and serene though it was, her mind insisted on thinking about Ryan.

Caroline sighed, knowing she would have to give in to her thoughts, knowing she couldn't keep Ryan out of her head after what she had learned. But if she had to think about him, then maybe she could at least control what she thought about. She settled on a memory from their senior year of high school. A happy time.

A time that, more and more, seemed like it belonged to someone else.

"So, you really don't know who Ryan is signing with today?" Chelsea Horton looked over at Caroline's reflection in the high school bathroom mirror.

Caroline shook her head, running her fingers through her blond hair, making sure it lay straight around her shoulders. "No. We agreed early on that we weren't going to tell each other which schools we were talking to. We didn't want to influence each other's decisions. We need to make our choices individually, without worrying about each other."

"When you say 'we,' do you mean 'he?'" McKenzie Thompson questioned her. Chelsea laughed as she pulled her lip gloss out of her bag. In just a few minutes, the three of them, along with a few boys from the baseball team, would be signing their letters of intent for the schools they would play for in college. A large group, including their families and friends and reporters for the local newspaper, had gathered in the school's cafeteria to celebrate.

"No, I don't just mean 'he.'" Caroline sighed in frustration. "We agreed on this."

"It's just so weird. You guys have been together almost two years. It seems like you'd consider your relationship in this decision." Chelsea clicked the cap back on her lip gloss.

"But we're only in high school," Caroline argued. "We wanted to make sure we chose based on the best opportunities for our education, and to play, without adding each other into the mix."

"I guess it kinda makes sense, when you put it that way." McKenzie tossed her auburn curls down her back. "You guys ready?"

"Yep." Chelsea threw her bag over her shoulder.

"Me, too." Caroline looked in the mirror one last time, making sure her jacket covered her t-shirt underneath. She and Ryan had also agreed to tell each other which college they were going to in private, before signing their letters. She didn't want to give it away before they were ready.

The girls turned the corner out of the bathroom and headed for the cafeteria. Caroline saw Ryan leaning against the wall, just outside the entrance. When he saw her, he stood up, his eyes full of anticipation.

"We'll see you in there, girl." Chelsea and McKenzie rushed ahead, leaving Caroline alone with Ryan.

He closed the distance between them, taking one of her hands in his, his thumb rubbing the back of her hand. "You ready for this?"

"I guess so. It's now or never, right?"

Ryan laughed. "Yeah, I guess that's kind of true." He let go of her hand and lifted his fingers to the zipper of his own jacket. She followed his lead.

They both pulled on their zippers, taking their time in revealing which college they had chosen. Heat filled Caroline's cheeks as she recognized the red, navy, and white A on Ryan's shirt, realizing it matched the one she was wearing.

Ryan put his arms around her waist, lifting her off the ground, and spun her in a circle "This is incredible!"

She put her arms around his neck. "It's perfect."

"This is gonna be great. Can you feel it, babe? This is it. This is our future."

Caroline smiled as he kissed her, feeling as happy as she had when U of A had offered her a scholarship.

Ryan pulled away. "Come on, let's go celebrate." He took her hand, leading her to the cafeteria.

Pulling her into their forever.

Caroline turned the key in the ignition, shutting her car off. She pulled her phone from her pocket to send two texts. The first to her dad.

> 5:27 PM: I'm back in Tucson, stopped by campus. Will be home soon.

The second to Ryan.

5:28 PM: Where are you?

She got out of her car, sliding her Student ID card into the pocket of her jeans. She shut the door harder than she intended. She leaned against her car, waiting for his reply.

The phone buzzed in her hand, and her heart skipped a beat. But the answer was from her dad, not from Ryan.

Dad 5:33 PM: See you soon.

Caroline pressed down on the lock button, her phone clicking as the screen turned black. She shoved it into her pocket and pushed herself off the car. She had a good idea where Ryan was, supported by the fact that he hadn't replied.

Dusk was settling around her as she headed down the campus streets toward the gym. The temperature was dropping, sending goose bumps down her arms. Rubbing her hands over them, she wished she'd have thought to grab her jacket.

Caroline paused as she reached the first set of windows that looked into the gym. Sure enough, there was Ryan, surrounded by his teammates as he lifted weights. She forgot the chill of the air as seeing him reminded her of her plan.

She rushed down the sidewalk to the entrance, using her ID card to open the door. Pushing her way past people working out, she wound her way through the treadmills and bikes and other machines until she stood in front of Ryan and his friends. Their shirts were darkened by sweat, and they laughed at something Ryan had just said.

"Ryan." All of their eyes snapped up to her. At the sound of her voice, their laughter quickly died away.

"Hey, babe. What are you doing here?" A flash of panic went through Ryan's eyes as he spoke.

"We need to talk." Caroline crossed her arms as his friends smacked him on the back, asking him what he had done wrong. "Alone."

"Alright. But can it wait? I'm kinda in the middle of my workout here."

"No, it can't wait. If it could wait, do you really think I would have shown up here?"

"Fine." Standing up, Ryan brushed past her. She followed as he headed toward the bathrooms. He found a corner in the hallway, then turned to face her.

"What's going on, Caroline?" He spat the question at her.

"I need to know what you were thinking."

"What I was thinking? About what?"

"What you were thinking yesterday."

Caroline watched as recognition flickered across his face. "I see your little friend told you everything."

"Ryan, if you were worried about our relationship, why didn't you just talk to me? Why would you go to Connor?" Caroline tried to keep the anger out of her voice, but she heard it echoing as she finished her question.

"Wait, you're mad at me?" Ryan's face turned red as his own anger surfaced.

"Why wouldn't I be? You threatened to punch him out, that the only thing that kept you from doing it was your scholarship. I think I deserve to be mad here."

"Caroline, you're blind if you don't see that guy has feelings for you. I was just telling him to back off, because you have a boyfriend."

Ryan's words caught her off guard. Trying to refocus, she shook her head. "He's my partner, we were assigned to work together. There's nothing else going on, I swear to you."

"Yeah, that's what he told me, too. But I don't buy it, Caroline."

"Well, you should, because it's the truth. I've never lied to you before, so why would I now? You think I'm blind? Well, I've got news for you. You're the one who's blind. You don't notice or care about what I've been going through. Maybe it's my fault for not trying to talk to you, but I didn't want to ruin what you've got going, with the scouts and stuff. But I can only take so much baseball. Even tonight, you wanted to finish your workout before talking to me."

Ryan clenched his jaw. "I have goals, Caroline. That's something you used to understand. I'm over here trying to make it to the majors, so I don't have time to constantly worry about how you are. So, you can't play softball anymore. You've had months to wrap your head around it. It's time to just get over it."

Caroline's mouth fell open as his words hit her, stinging as much as if she'd been slapped. Tears found her eyes, but she fought them off. "Get over it? How, Ryan? Please tell me how to get over it because I'm dying to. Why don't you try putting yourself in my shoes for half a second? Listening to your boyfriend go on about his success, going to practice every day and watching girls take your place, watching them win and making you feel like your place on the team never even mattered. Always worrying about what future you could possibly have now that everything you ever worked for is gone? But please, explain to me how to just get over it."

Glaring at her, Ryan's green eyes grew dark and cold. "I don't know what you want me to do, Caroline."

She studied him, looking for any trace of sadness or

regret. Searching for any signs of an apology. But there was nothing in his face that she was looking for. There wasn't anything there that she recognized.

"I guess I don't want you to do anything." A tear slid down her cheek, and she swatted it away with her fingertips. "I think I need a break."

"A break." Ryan repeated her words, his expression unchanging.

"Yeah. This way you get all the time you need for baseball. You won't have to constantly worry about me anymore." She fought off more tears as she threw his own words back at him.

Ryan scoffed and rolled his eyes as he looked down at the floor. "Yeah, I think a break might be best. If you're done, I have a workout I need to get back to."

Caroline stared after him as he passed her in the hallway, not waiting for her answer. She bit her lip, but her tears broke free. She ducked her head, hiding her eyes from everyone in the crowded gym. She burst through the door, not looking up as she hurried toward her car. Her face was soaked, and the cool air chilled her cheeks as she went. But the freezing pain was easy to ignore.

Because it was nothing compared to the breaking of her heart.

Fourteen

THE EARLY AFTERNOON SUN SHONE THROUGH Caroline's window, its beams forming a crisscross of light over her bed. She was lying on her stomach across her comforter, studying the slides of the presentation she and Connor had put together the day before. She was doing her best to focus on the script, trying to remember what she was supposed to say with each slide, but her mind kept wandering.

Caroline sniffed and dabbed at her eyes for the hundredth time that day. She wasn't just crying because of breaking up with Ryan. So much had changed in the past few months, and it was all starting to catch up with her.

She jumped as there was a tap on her door. "Caroline, honey? Can I come in?" Her dad turned the handle, creaking it open a little.

"Just a second." Slamming her laptop shut, she hid the PowerPoint and script filled with horses. She still hadn't told her parents she was taking the weanling class. "Alright, all set." She sat up and pushed herself to the edge of her bed.

Doug entered the room, holding a tray with a bowl and a glass on it. "How about some homemade macaroni and cheese and a chocolate milkshake?"

"Sounds great. But what's the occasion?"

Her dad looked down to the carpet. "Well, I thought

they might help your broken heart?"

"Who said I have a broken heart?"

He cleared his throat and looked at the circle of tissues surrounding her on the bed. Caroline followed his eyes. "Oh. Right."

Doug took a few steps and sat down near her, putting the tray between them. "I told your mom how you came home last night, without eating and never coming out of your room. She figured something happened and told me to try this, since she's at the horse show and can't."

Caroline smiled a little as her dad spoke. "I was wondering how you figured it out on your own." She reached for the glass and sipped through the straw, savoring the flavor and the coldness as the ice cream slid down her dry throat. "That's really good, Dad. Thank you."

"You're welcome." He stared down at her blankets. "Do you wanna tell me what happened?"

Caroline sighed and pulled her fingers through her bangs. "Ryan and I...we decided to take a break."

"What happened?"

"I guess it's been building for quite a while. He's so obsessed with baseball right now, with all these scouts calling him. It's all he talks about and it's just hard for me." Caroline sniffed. "He doesn't ask how I'm feeling or notice what's going on with me. And it's probably my fault more than his for not trying to tell him how I've been feeling, but I didn't want to take away from what he's got going on. He should be excited, but that doesn't make it any easier for me." Caroline paused to take a breath.

"Did you try telling him how you're feeling?"

Caroline nodded. "Yeah. He told me he didn't have time to constantly worry about how I am because he has goals, and how that was something I used to understand. He also told me I should be over the fact that I can't play anymore 'cause it's been months since I got hurt." She sniffed and worked to hold in the tears that stung her eyes.

"Seriously? He said all that?" Doug shook his head in disbelief.

"Yeah, he did." Caroline bit her lip, debating whether to tell her dad about Ryan's threat toward Connor, but decided against it. She didn't want to talk about Connor, or the weanling class.

"I liked that kid a lot, and he is a good ballplayer, but that's not how you treat people. Especially someone you've been dating for as long as you two have."

Caroline nodded as she picked up the fork and speared a few noodles. "We're just in different places. Everything in the world is going right for him, and he's never been more certain of his future. He can't relate to me." She popped the macaroni into her mouth.

"But he should still show he cares about you. You'd think he could imagine what it'd be like if it had happened to him."

Caroline shrugged and focused on chewing.

Doug shook his head. "Enough about him. What are you gonna do now?"

She looked down at her computer. "Well, I have some more studying to do before classes tomorrow."

"I don't mean right now, silly girl."

She squinted at her dad and tilted her head sideways. "What do you mean then?"

"I mean in general." He looked her in the eyes, a gentle smile on his face. "You're not playing, you quit as manager, you broke up with Ryan. I'm just wondering if you have a plan."

"Um, no. I guess I don't have a plan. Besides getting

through these classes this semester." Caroline stared down at the fork in her hand, memorizing the pattern etched in the silver.

"That's alright. That's a lot of change for someone to go through in such a short amount of time. You don't need to have anything figured out yet. But are you handling it all okay? Your mom and I are worried about you."

She lifted her eyes to his. "You guys don't need to worry. I'm fine."

Her dad raised her eyebrows at her, eyeing the tissues once again. "I'm not sure I believe you."

Caroline rolled her eyes. "Alright, maybe not in this exact moment. But overall, I'm fine."

Doug smiled sideways. "Fair enough. Just know we're here, okay?"

Caroline nodded her head. "I know, Dad. I appreciate it."

He reached over and squeezed her hand. "Good. Well, I'll let you get back to studying. Holler if you need anything." He stood up and took a few steps to the door.

"Hey, Dad?"

"Yeah?" He turned back to face her, his hand on the doorknob.

"Thank you."

Doug smiled at her. "No problem, kiddo."

As the door clicked shut, Caroline stood up, stretching her arms up over head. She rolled her right shoulder in a few circles, working out the tension and tightness that had built up. She turned toward her window and looked out over the trail-covered fields. A few horses and riders were headed out, reminding Caroline of another time she had worried her parents. Another time, years ago, that she had caused them concern, but under completely different circumstances.

The skin on her cheeks stretched under her smile. The cool breeze reminded her more of the winter that was leaving than of the spring that was coming, but the abundant sunshine was strong enough to keep her warm. Beau's breathing was in rhythm with the step of his canter and his hooves padded the grass of the field beneath them. All too soon, the fence line came into view, signaling they were almost home.

"Whoa, bud," Caroline breathed out as she shifted her weight and gave a light pull on the reins, asking her horse to walk. Beau snorted and tossed his head, resisting her request. Caroline laughed and asked him again.

This time Beau listened. As Caroline slid the reins through her fingers to give him his head, he sighed. "I know, big guy. I could've gone a lot longer, too, but we better get back." She pointed him toward the gate that led back to the barn.

Caroline kicked her feet out of the stirrups as they strolled through the field, rolling her ankles in circles. She ran her fingers through his mane, smiling at how far they had come.

They had made the move up to preliminary last year, and in just two weeks, they would make their one-star debut. Caroline was excited for the challenge and happy they were one step closer to her goal of competing at the Young Rider Championships that summer.

Her phone buzzed from the pocket of her light jacket. She put the reins into one hand, working the zipper and pulling her phone to where she could see it with the other. Four missed calls and twice as many texts from her mom.

She read the last one first.

> Mom, 3:33 PM: Getting really
> worried. Going to tack up and come
> look for you.

Caroline's eyes focused on the time typed out next to the text. She had been out riding for over two hours. "Oops. We were gone way too long, bud." She sent a quick text back.

> 3:34 PM: Sorry. Almost home.

She locked her phone and slid it back into her pocket. She picked up the reins and her stirrups but didn't ask Beau to go faster than a walk. He needed to cool down before they got to the barn.

Reaching the top of the last hill, she could see the front of the barn. Its white paint was welcoming, with large flower pots hanging down from the front beam. Her mom and her dad were standing near the doorway, waiting for her, both of them waving as they approached.

Caroline stopped Beau a few feet from the barn. She swung her right leg over his back and dropped to the ground. She barely got her stirrups pulled up before her mom was giving her a hug.

"Caroline, honey, what happened? You were gone for so long. We were so worried."

Hugging her back, Caroline worked to keep one hand holding on to Beau. "Nothing happened, Mom. I just lost track of time."

Her mom looked at her, blinking twice. "But you didn't answer your phone."

"I didn't hear it or feel it. We were having such a nice ride. I'm sorry."

"You have to be the only fourteen-year-old girl in the world who doesn't notice when her phone goes off." Her dad stepped forward and put an arm around his wife.

"Yeah, but is that really a bad thing?" Caroline smiled as Beau lifted his head and blew into her ear.

Her parents looked at each other before laughing. "No, I guess it isn't. Come on, let's go get this guy untacked." Her mom reached out and stroked Beau on the shoulder as Caroline led him into the barn.

Caroline blinked and tore herself away from the window. Finding a clean tissue, she wiped at the tears running down her cheeks, then opened her laptop to resume her homework. Focusing on school might distract her from the pain she was feeling.

And it would keep her from wondering if she would ever find a way to be that happy again.

Fifteen

CONNOR COULD TELL IT HADN'T GONE WELL as soon as she walked into the classroom. Caroline's eyes were red and puffy, and her face was pale. She didn't look like she had slept at all since he had seen her on Saturday. But since she had slipped into her seat seconds before class started, he would have to wait to find out any details.

Caroline pulled out her notebook and wrote the date across the top. Even though they were listening to presentations all week, they still had to take notes. They would be tested on the material their peers taught them.

Connor did his best to focus on his classmates and their presentation, but every time he heard Caroline sniff, he got more anxious. Looking at her through the corner of his eye, he saw her hand shaking, not quite the trembling she had shown at the beginning of the semester, but enough to change her neat handwriting into soft scribble.

Without taking his eyes away from the students presenting, he tore off a small corner of his paper. *Are you ok?* he printed in little letters. He slid the note to her until it touched her elbow. Caroline looked down. She reached for the paper, bringing it closer with her fingers. She blinked twice, adjusting her eyes so she could read the small print.

Caroline lifted her eyes to his. One side of her mouth lifted in an attempt to smile as she shrugged her shoulders. Connor nodded his head in reply as Caroline folded the note and stuck it into the pocket at the front of her binder.

Connor sighed as he refocused on the presentation at the front of the room. She wasn't okay, that much was obvious, but they didn't have time to talk about it, and they couldn't keep passing notes. They needed to pay attention.

As Kaitlin and Maddie wrapped up their presentation on Clinton Anderson, Dr. Carnes reached into his ball cap to pull out the names of the next presenters. Connor crossed his fingers, hoping it wouldn't be their turn. He could tell Caroline could use a few more days before standing up in front of a room full of people.

"Thank you, girls. Well done," Dr. Carnes spoke as he wrote one last note down on his grading sheet. "Does anyone have any questions for them?" No one raised their hand.

"Alright then, next up we will have Connor and Caroline. Let's take a five-minute break to let them get ready." Dr. Carnes looked to where they were seated, and Connor felt his stomach drop. A few of their classmates stood, their chairs screeching across the floor as they headed outside for the short break.

Caroline clicked her pen and set it down on her notebook, bending over to pull out her index cards from her bag on the floor. Connor cleared his throat. "Caroline, do you want me to ask Dr. Carnes if we could go later in the week? I could tell him you're not feeling well."

Caroline turned back around to face him, the index cards wobbling in her shaky hands. "I'm okay," she swallowed. "We better go ahead and do it, so he doesn't take points off for not being ready."

"I'm not worried about the points, if you need time."

"I appreciate that, but I'll be okay." Caroline tried to smile as she nodded her head.

"Alright, let's do it then." Connor reached down to his backpack and pulled out his own cards and his flash drive. Together they walked to the front of the classroom.

Connor squatted down so he was even with the computer on the table, plugged the flash drive in, and waited for it to open up. He found their PowerPoint and called it up, selecting the slideshow option. Standing, he made eye contact with Caroline. "Ready?"

"Yep." Again, Caroline tried to smile.

Connor smiled back at her while their classmates settled back into their seats. He nodded his head at Caroline, encouraging her to begin.

Caroline opened her mouth to talk, but only a small sound came out. *Lord, give her strength to get through this. Help me help her, whatever that may look like.* Connor shifted his weight toward her, debating if he should take over for the first slide. Before he could do anything, Caroline closed her eyes and took a deep breath. When she looked back at him, her entire expression had changed. Her face shone with a confidence he hadn't seen in her before.

"Pat Parelli utilizes seven games as the foundation of his training program. He developed these games by watching horses interact with each other. He uses them to establish trust and acceptance with the horse, and to improve communication between horse and handler." Caroline looked over to Connor, nodding her head, indicating to him that he could move on to the next slide.

Connor hit the next button, trying to hide the shock he was feeling for how Caroline had pulled herself together. Hesitating, he took a moment to put his thoughts in order, as it was his turn to speak. "The first of these seven games is the Friendly Game. The purpose of this game is to get the horse used to your presence and to get him comfortable with you touching him." Connor clicked on the screen, playing a video Caroline had recorded of him playing the Friendly Game with one of the horses at his ranch. Caroline described everything he was doing as the video played.

Her confidence stayed throughout the whole presentation. Before Connor knew it, their required fifteen minutes passed, and they were headed back to their seats. Reaching their table, he had to fight himself to keep from giving her a hug.

"I'd say that went well," Connor picked up his pen and adjusted his notebook.

Glancing at him, Caroline took a drink out of her water bottle. "Yeah," she said after she swallowed. "I'm sorry for how it started though." The tired sadness had returned to her eyes.

"No need to be sorry. It all worked out." Connor studied her, wondering if he could ask how she did it. He opened his mouth, but Dr. Carnes's voice rang out instead.

"Alright, gang, we don't really have time for another one today, so let's get an early start on lab. Grab halters, lead ropes, and brush buckets, and we'll meet at the pasture gate."

Connor slapped his notebook closed and scooted his chair back. "You wanna grab the brush bucket and I'll grab the halter?" he asked Caroline as he packed his stuff and stood.

Caroline was moving a little slower than he was, not as eager to get outside. "Sure." She closed her binder as Connor headed out the door, in a rush to get to talk to her.

He grabbed the soft, light-pink halter they had been using on Luna and pulled the white cotton lead rope off the hanger. He clipped the snap to the ring at the bottom of the halter, pausing for just a moment to catch his breath.

Connor had been in such a hurry, he was the first one to reach the pasture. All of the babies were grazing, the fall breeze lifting the ends of their tails. Connor clucked his tongue against the roof of his mouth. Two heads popped up, their black and red coats glistening in the sun. With ears perked forward, Luna and Rebel came trotting to him.

Rebel reached him first, but only by two steps. Luna pushed her way past him and put her head over the gate. Connor extended his palm, and Luna leaned forward to lick it.

"Hi, pretty girl. Can you do me a favor?" Connor spoke under his breath as the filly continued to search his hand with her tongue. "Caroline is having a rough time today, so can you try your hardest to be on your best behavior?"

Luna sighed and shook her entire body, freeing a small cloud of tan dust from her coat. Connor smiled. "I'll take that as a yes."

Several voices diverted his attention back toward the barn. He glanced over his shoulder and saw the rest of the class coming. Everyone walked with their partner, chatting and laughing, except for Caroline. She was in the back, her eyes down at the ground. Connor regretted rushing out on her. *Lord, help me be a friend to her. Show me what she needs.*

Dr. Carnes walked to the front of the group and opened the gate. "Alright, everybody. Let's get all of the weanlings caught and take them over to the dry lot by the barn. We'll continue working on the trail course, and I want all of them to get a good grooming today. The nights are starting to get colder, and we want to make sure their coats are clean, so they stay warm."

Caroline stayed in the back of the group as Connor went in and haltered Luna. As they walked to the dry lot,

Caroline fell into step beside them.

Connor swallowed, then cleared his throat. "I'm sorry I was in such a hurry in the classroom. I didn't mean to make you walk by yourself."

One side of Caroline's mouth lifted. "Oh, no worries. I didn't even give it a second thought. No need to be sorry. I'm fine."

Connor turned his head and raised his eyebrows at her.

Caroline chuckled. "Alright. Maybe I'm not fine. But I meant we're fine."

"Fair enough," Connor laughed as they passed through the gate to the dry lot. "What do you think, should we groom her first? Then practice the trail course?"

"Sure, sounds good."

They walked Luna over to the barn and found a place out of the way of the trail course. Caroline set the brush bucket down on the ground behind Connor and grabbed a round curry comb. She slid the strap over her hand and approached Luna's shoulder. She reached out, touching the filly with her bare hand first, before applying the curry. As she started rubbing Luna's coat in a circular motion, the young horse leaned into her touch. Connor studied Caroline's face. The sadness and tension started to leave her with every circle she made on Luna's coat.

Connor rubbed the crescent moon on Luna's forehead. "Caroline, can I ask you something?"

Caroline lifted her eyes to his as she continued working on Luna's coat. "Yeah, go ahead."

"Back in the classroom, when we started our presentation, it seemed like you couldn't do it. You started to talk, but nothing came out. Then all of a sudden, you flipped a switch, and you were fine." Connor paused, taking a breath.

Caroline stared at him. "I guess I'm waiting for a question?"

Connor laughed. "Right. Well, I guess I'm just wondering how you did it."

A slight hint of red came across Caroline's cheeks as she looked back down to Luna's coat. "If I tell you, you'll either laugh at me, or think I'm crazy."

Connor grinned. "What if I promise to do neither?"

Caroline rolled her eyes. "I don't think you can make that promise."

"I think I can. I won't laugh. I just want to know."

Caroline looked at him, her eyes doubtful, her cheeks still red. "Alright, I'll hold you to that." She slid the curry comb off her hand and reached for the lead rope. "Do you want to get her other side?"

"Sure thing." Connor handed her the rope as he slid the curry over his own hand. He started working at Luna's shoulder.

Caroline sighed, running her fingers through Luna's forelock. "In high school softball, we were the Colts. That was our mascot. Our coach put a horseshoe on the wall by the entrance to the bullpen. When we got to the field for practice or a game, we would touch it. It was our way of leaving everything from our day outside, so we could focus on what we needed to do. Just a little mental trick. Obviously, I needed to focus on our presentation, so I pictured the horseshoe and touched it in my head."

Connor watched as her cheeks turned a deeper red. Caroline wouldn't look up at him. She just kept running her fingers through Luna's forelock. "Hey, I'm not laughing," Connor reassured her as he put the curry comb away and reached for the stiff bristled brush.

"True, but you have to think I'm crazy."

"No, not at all." Connor began to work Luna's coat with the brush. "That's an important memory to you, and it's still something that works now. There's nothing crazy about that."

Caroline looked up then, her head tilted sideways, some of the red disappearing from her face. A slight smile crossed her lips. "Thank you."

"You're welcome." Connor stepped around Luna's shoulder and passed Caroline the brush, taking the lead from her as they switched places. "Can I ask you something else?"

Caroline chuckled. "Sure."

"What happened with Ryan?"

"I figured that was coming." Caroline flicked her wrist a couple of times as she brushed Luna's shoulder. She took a deep breath, then let all of the air come out in a rush from her mouth. "We decided to take a break."

"So, things didn't go well?"

"No, not really." Caroline paused from brushing Luna and met Connor's eyes. "I really am sorry about what he did."

"You have nothing to be sorry for. He did it, not you."

"But it was my fault. I've changed, and he doesn't know how to take it." She looked away, refocusing on Luna's coat.

Connor studied her again, watching her face and eyes as she brushed Luna's rump. He couldn't decide whether or not to ask his next question. Caroline turned to him, handing him the brush. "I think we can clean her hooves now."

Connor took the brush from her and gave her the rope. Bending down, he pulled the hoof pick from the bucket. When he straightened, Caroline had a small smirk on her face.

"What?"

"You can go ahead and ask."

Connor felt shock work its way into his face. "How'd you know I have another question?"

"Just an observation." Caroline dropped her eyes, pulling on stray strands of cotton hanging from the lead rope. "It's getting pretty easy to read you."

"Good to know." Connor hoped his face wasn't as red as it felt. "So, I can ask?"

Caroline nodded her head.

"How have you changed?" Connor turned his back to her, bending down to pick up Luna's foot.

Caroline sighed. "I'm not the softball girl anymore. I'm trying to move on."

Connor set Luna's hoof back down on the ground and turned to face her. "For what it's worth, I think you're allowed to do that."

Caroline pressed her lips together, studying him. "Why do you say that?"

Connor cleared his throat. "I just mean you've dealt with a lot and you've lost a lot. I think it only makes sense to try to move on."

Her eyes shined with tears as she blinked, nodding her head in agreement.

Connor moved to Luna's back foot, cleaning out all the dirt. "Wanna get the other two, then start working on the trail course?"

"Yeah, sure."

Luna stood still while Caroline finished her hooves. Tossing the hoof pick back into the bucket, she came around to the filly's head. Stroking her nose with one finger, she sniffed.

"You okay?" Connor watched her as he spoke.

"Trying to be." Caroline looked out to the lot, eyeing the obstacles. "Think we should start with backing through the L today?"

"Sounds like a plan to me. Do you want me to take her first?"

"I'd like to, if that's okay." Caroline looked up at him, tears still brimming in her eyes.

"Yeah, go for it." Connor handed her the lead rope and followed them to the L-shaped chute.

It was the least scary obstacle on the course, but one of the most challenging. They had to walk the horse through the L, then back them out without their feet stepping onto or over any of the poles. It was all about control and communication, two things Caroline made seem easy.

Her timing was perfect as she used her hand on the rope and her body to tell Luna when to back up, and when to start making the turn. Luna's ears flicked back and forth as she listened, moving her feet with care. As they cleared the end of the last pole, Caroline looked over to Connor, grinning from ear to ear.

Connor grinned back, his own smile filling his face as he couldn't help but wonder if he and Luna were the reason Caroline was starting to move on.

And he couldn't help but let that wonder turn into a sense of hope.

Sixteen

CAROLINE COULDN'T STARE AT THE WALLS ANY LONGER. Saturday had just started, but already she had finished her homework, done some laundry, and washed dishes. There was nothing else for her to do.

Except argue with herself.

She kept glancing at the phone in her hand, her fingers hovering over the screen as she went back and forth over whether or not to send the text.

She had nothing to do. What would it hurt to ask Connor about coming over? He had said she could whenever she wanted to.

But why would she go? What would they do if they didn't have a project to work on?

Caroline sighed. She couldn't remember the last Saturday she didn't have something going on. Between softball and horses, she had always been busy.

She looked down at the barn from where she sat in her window seat, knees to her chest. Wrapping her arms around them, she laid her cheek against her knees. She could see her dad on the tractor, spreading manure across the back fields. Her mom was in the arena, setting jumps for her lessons that day. Everyone had something to do, a purpose.

Everyone but her.

As the familiar ache spoke up in her heart, her phone buzzed, alerting her of a text message. She opened it to find a picture from Connor.

> Connor, 8:03 AM: Nothing says
> Saturday like a new can of paint!
> What are you up to today?

Her fingers typed her response before she let her head talk her out of it.

> 8:04 AM: Nothing. Want some help
> painting?

Caroline held her breath, staring at her phone as she waited for his response. She grinned as his message lit up her screen.

> Connor, 8:05 AM: Yeah! You
> remember how to get here?

> 8:05 AM: I do! See you soon!

Standing up from the window seat, she stretched before heading to her closet. She found an old, long-sleeve t-shirt and an old pair of jeans. She pulled her ponytail through a baseball cap and headed for the stairs. She took them one step at a time, texting her parents as she went to let them know she was leaving.

Caroline grabbed her purse from the counter and reached for her keys from the rack by the cabinet, jumping as something vibrated beneath it. She looked down, seeing both of her parent's phones lying there. Sighing at the sight of her own text, she turned away and headed for the door.

She put her purse and keys into the front seat of her

car and looked toward the barn again. A few horses and riders were now circling around her mom, warming up before they started jumping. Her dad was somewhere on the other side of the property, out of her sight.

Caroline bit her lip, debating whether her text was enough, or if she should go tell her mom she was leaving. She pushed herself away from her car, knowing it would be hours before either of her parents checked their phones.

It was a short walk to the arena fence, where she waited, arms crossed, for her mom to see her.

"Now this time when you ask for the canter, make sure you open up your hip. If you close it, he can't step up with his back leg, and the transition won't be as smooth," Holly instructed.

Caroline's eyes zoomed in on the horse and rider. The girl's lips were pressed together as she focused, trying to make her body do the right things.

Caroline could remember that kind of focus, the struggle to get everything in the right place at the right time. Timing was everything, in horses, and in softball.

Sweat trickled down her neck as Caroline reset her feet on the rubber. She lifted her eyes to her dad, who was sitting on a bucket at home plate, ready to catch her next pitch. They'd been at it for over an hour.

Doug lifted his glove, asking for her fastball to cross the inside corner of the plate. She nodded her head, spun the ball around in her glove as she felt for the seams, and then started her motion. She used every inch of her strength to deliver the pitch, but her right elbow collided with her hip as she tried to snap her wrist. She bent over at the waist, from pain and frustration.

"If you get your hips open and out of the way, that doesn't happen." Her dad chuckled. "You okay?"

"Yeah, I'm fine." Caroline straightened as he tossed the ball back to her. "What was the speed on that one?"

"Fifty-nine." Holly stood behind Doug, radar gun in hand. Caroline's goal for the day was to hit sixty.

Caroline took a deep breath as she set her feet once again, refocusing on what she needed to do.

"Get your hips open, so they can pop, and so everything can be on time." Her dad encouraged her as he lifted his glove. He wanted the ball in the same spot as the previous pitch.

Finding her grip, Caroline began her delivery. This time, she could tell from the moment her left foot touched the ground that her hips were in the right spot and that everything was on time. All of this was confirmed when the ball smacked into her dad's glove in the exact location he wanted it, the sound echoing across their backyard.

Caroline grinned as her dad turned to look at her mom. She turned the radar gun so he could read it. When he turned back to Caroline, his grin was as big as hers.

"What was it?"

"Sixty-two."

"Seriously?"

"Seriously."

Caroline jogged to them, wanting to see the radar gun for herself. Sure enough, the numbers showed that her pitch had traveled that fast.

"Good job, honey." Her mom smiled at her, but Caroline noticed that her smile didn't quite reach her eyes.

"Caroline, honey, what's wrong? Did you need

something?" Holly called to her from the arena, her eyes wide with surprise.

Caroline blinked, the moisture in her eyes surprising her. She swallowed, clearing her throat of her tears. "I, uh, just wanted to tell you I'm leaving for a while. I should be back before dinner, though."

Caroline saw her mom's shoulders relax. "Oh. When I saw you there, I thought...never mind." She shook her head and tried to smile. "Hope you have a good time." Holly waved as she turned back to her students. Walking away, Caroline ambled to her car.

Her mom's face stayed with her, forcing her to stop at her car door. She hadn't been down to the arena or the barns in years. No wonder her mom had been surprised.

But what was sticking out in her mind was the hope she had seen.

Holding the handle, Caroline hesitated, looking back at her mom. Holly's attention had returned to her students. Caroline bit her lip, as she fought with the pull in her heart to go back to the arena. To climb up to the top rail of the fence and sit down to watch, like she had so many times before. Like she hadn't in so long.

But Connor was expecting her. Opening her door, she climbed in, leaving a plume of dust as she pulled away.

It wasn't until she took the exit off the interstate to Sonoita that Caroline felt herself release the tension in her shoulders. She sighed and tried to enjoy the scenery around her.

But her mind wouldn't let her. She kept seeing her mom's face, the hope from this morning, and the forced smile whenever it came to softball.

Their relationship had changed after her accident, and it had never recovered. Caroline knew her mom loved her, and supported her, but she would always have to live with the disappointment and hurt she had caused her mom by not riding again.

She would never forget the last time they had talked about horses. It had been a few months after the accident, a few weeks since her parents had shown her the for-sale ads in the barn. Caroline was in the kitchen working on homework, when her mom came in.

"Hey, honey, can I show you a video?"

Caroline nodded and pushed her homework aside. She glanced down at her mom's phone, gulping as she saw the horse.

The blood bay gelding was jumping, and it was easy to see how talented he was. And how much he loved his job. Caroline watched with some interest, but a knot formed in the center of her stomach.

"He's great, isn't he?" her mom had asked as the video ended. "His name is Northern Tranquility. He's only done a couple shows at training level, but he is super brave, and it won't be hard for you to move him up the levels."

"Me?" Caroline had croaked out.

"Oh. I guess I skipped that part. Yeah, we bought him for you."

The knot in her stomach turned over, changing from nerves to frustration. "I told you I didn't want another horse."

"Caroline, you say that now, and I get it, but that'll pass. He was too talented to let go."

"It's not going to pass. I don't want a horse."

Her mom's tone had changed from pleading to angry. "Caroline, I can't stand by and let you throw it all away. I wouldn't be doing my job as your mother, as your teacher, if I let you give in to fear."

"It's not fear, Mom!" Caroline stood up as her mom interrupted her.

"Yes, it is! You had an awful wreck, and you've waited too long to get back on."

"I've waited too long? How do you suggest I could have sped up the process? Without a horse, and with being laid up in the hospital?" Caroline clenched her fists.

"That's why I bought this horse, Caroline. To get you back out there." Holly's lips pushed together into a straight line.

"Can you just listen to me, please? I don't want a horse and I don't want to ride anymore! I'm done!" Caroline had screamed, then ran up the stairs before her tears, or her mom's, had become visible.

They hadn't talked about horses or riding since.

Caroline sighed, adjusting the air conditioning as she drove up the last hill before Connor's road. She still felt guilty for yelling at her mom. She could've handled it better. Or she could've done something in the five years that had passed to make up for it. To fix it.

Pulling into Connor's driveway, something else occurred to her. A thought that had never crossed her mind before.

She had never asked what happened to that horse.

Seventeen

CAROLINE DID HER BEST TO CLEAR HER THOUGHTS as she stepped out of her car. She stretched her arms over her head, taking in the fields dotted with horses. Blue came trotting over to greet her.

Kneeling down, she scratched the old dog behind his ears. His eyes lit up and he licked her cheek.

"How you doin', bud?" His tail wagged, beating the ground with his reply.

"He really likes you." Connor walked up from behind her, two bottles of water in hand.

Caroline gave Blue one last pat before she straightened, turning to Connor. "Well, I really like him, too."

Connor grinned. "Here, this is for you." He handed her one of the water bottles. "Ready to get started?"

"Sure. What are we painting?"

"The stallion barn." Connor began walking. "We're getting ready for our annual open house in a couple of weeks."

Caroline tried to ignore the knot that formed in her stomach. *You've been in the barn before. And you were fine. Just breathe.* "Why do you do it in the fall?"

"We're so busy in the spring, with foaling out mares and breeding, we don't really have time. Not to mention we don't really want people all over the place when we've got brand-new babies on the ground. And it gives clients a chance to think about which stallion they want to breed to."

Caroline nodded her head. "Makes sense."

They walked into the barn, where a few cans of paint, brushes, and a stepladder were all set up.

"I thought I could work on the trim, if you want to work on the walls and stall doors. Or vice versa, whichever you prefer." Connor squatted down next to the cans, prying one open.

Caroline nodded her head as she looked down the aisle. Most of the stallions were snoozing in the corners of their stalls. Jasper had his head over the door, looking at her. She smiled to herself, remembering how sweet he was from her last visit. She stepped over to him, her heart fluttering as he nickered at her.

"He remembers you," Connor commented as he walked up behind her.

"Maybe." Caroline lifted her hand to the gray stallion. He placed his nuzzle in her palm, blowing warm air through her fingers.

"No maybes there." Connor smiled as their eyes met.

"Hey, Connor?" Boot heels clicked on the concrete of the barn aisle as both Connor and Caroline turned in the direction of the voice.

Caroline could tell this was Connor's mom. Her brown eyes, light brown hair, and smile reflected what Caroline saw in Connor. At her smile, Caroline couldn't help but smile back.

"You must be Caroline. It's nice to meet you." Before Caroline could speak, she pulled her into a hug.

"Mom." Connor cleared his throat as she let Caroline go.

"What? You know I'm a hugger."

"You're right, I do, but Caroline doesn't."

"Right. I guess I should apologize." She shrugged her shoulders. Connor rolled his eyes as Caroline laughed.

"It's alright, Mrs. Taylor. I'm a hugger, too."

"Well, good! You'll fit right in around here, then. But please, call me Jessica."

Caroline nodded, a small smile across her lips.

"Anyway, Connor, is it okay if I borrow you for a moment? I need to get some boxes down from the top shelf in the office in the breeding barn, and I can't reach them."

"Of course." Connor looked to Caroline. "Do you want to tag along, or stay here?"

Jasper snorted at her, just as Connor asked. They all laughed. "I think I'll stay here. Jasper seems to think he needs a bit more attention."

Connor grinned at her. "Alright, sounds good. I won't be too long, okay?"

"Okay, I'll be fine."

Caroline turned her attention back to Jasper as Connor and his mom disappeared down the barn aisle. The sweet stallion nickered at her again, as if he was thanking her for staying.

"You're welcome, big guy," she whispered. She stroked his nose, breathing in as she savored the soft velvet feel of his muzzle in her hand.

Caroline closed her eyes, fighting back the tears that threatened to fall down her cheeks. Her heart ached for everything she had turned away from.

And from the longing to find a way back.

At a sudden crash from behind her, Caroline spun around with a gasp. The noise came from the last stall across the aisle.

Caroline eyed the nameplate from where she stood. The Lighthouse. Images of the abused chestnut horse she had seen Connor's dad unload from the trailer the last time she was there danced in front of her eyes. Her chest tightened as she tried to breathe. With everything that had happened with Ryan, she hadn't remembered to ask Connor about him. But it was obvious Edison hadn't improved much.

With small steps, Caroline tiptoed away from Jasper's stall, hoping for just a peek of Edison. He cowered in the back corner of his stall, pawing at the floor, his skin stretched taut over every rigid muscle in his body.

Caroline stopped three feet from the door. She peered over it on her tiptoes, seeing his grain bucket smashed against the wall, bent almost in half from the dent in the middle of it.

"Well, that wasn't very smart, bud. What are you going to eat out of, now that you kicked your bucket?" Caroline muttered. Edison continued to paw.

Even under the patches of dirt and loose, dull hair, and the knots in his mane and tail, it was easy to see how beautiful he was. The copper red of his coat was highlighted by the blond of his mane. The angles of his haunches and shoulders were perfect, and his muscles showed off his athletic structure.

"No one here is going to hurt you. You have to know that by now." Caroline took two steps closer to the stall. At the sound of her voice, Edison's head snapped up and he froze, his eyes looking straight into hers.

Caroline's breath caught in her throat. The connection she felt with him was so familiar. The pain and fear in his eyes reflected what she often felt herself. Without thinking, she closed the space between her and the door, reaching out and touching the top of it with her fingers.

She didn't move or make a sound as Edison came closer. She watched his face, making sure he didn't pin his ears or bare his teeth. But his expression stayed curious; his eyes showed nothing but hope.

Edison stretched his neck toward Caroline, until the tip of his nose touched her fingers. He snorted, jumping back, startled by the contact.

Caroline did her best not to react. She forced herself to sigh, releasing the tension from her neck. "Hey, I promise I won't hurt you. You can come back." She rested her forearms on the top of the door, the rough wood snagging the sleeves of her shirt. She turned her hand over, laying her palm face up for the horse.

Edison looked into her eyes again, blinking twice as he thought about coming closer. He took a couple of steps before stretching out his neck again. This time when he touched her, he didn't jump back.

He sighed, licking his lips as he took another step toward her. Caroline held still as he placed his chin in her hand.

"That's a good boy." She lifted her other hand, being careful not to startle him. He watched her hand but didn't move. Extending her fingers, she rested them on the perfect white diamond on his face. She rubbed his forehead, freeing loose hair from under his forelock. Closing his eyes, Edison leaned into her touch.

Caroline heard footsteps coming down the aisle. She turned her head, meeting Connor's eyes as he and Jessica approached. They slowed their steps, their faces full of questions.

"Caroline?" Connor kept his voice quiet. "How did you...?" His voice trailed off.

She shrugged her shoulders. "I didn't really do anything. I just stood here, and he came to me."

"That's amazing." Jessica looked from Caroline, to Edison, back to Caroline. "Would you try grooming him? He's such a mess, and none of us has been able to go near him."

"Mom, maybe that's not a good idea. Maybe we shouldn't push it." Connor looked at Caroline, his voice full of concern for her.

"Um, Connor, it's okay. I'd like to try." Caroline tried to sound convincing even as she heard her voice wobble.

Connor blinked, surprise shining in his eyes. "Are you sure?"

Caroline nodded.

"Well, okay, let me go grab some brushes. Connor, will you hand her his halter?" Jessica headed back down the barn aisle.

Connor reached beside Caroline for the leather halter on the hanger, keeping his movements slow. "Caroline, you don't have to do this." Connor unbuckled the halter and handed it to her.

Caroline took her hand off Edison's forehead to take the halter from Connor. "I know I don't. But look at him. He needs it."

"Alright." Connor sighed. "But be careful."

"I will. And you'll be here. Just like in class." Caroline lifted her lips in a small smile, looking at Connor over her shoulder.

Connor rolled his eyes, his smile matching hers. "Fair enough."

Caroline reached for the latch on the stall door, trying to be quiet as she worked the metal. "Hey, bud. It's just me. I'm gonna come in, okay?"

Edison tensed as Caroline pulled the door open just far enough to slip inside. She stopped just inside the stall door as he moved away from her, the whites of his eyes showing.

"It's okay," Caroline told herself as much as she was telling Edison. "It's just like before. I'm gonna be right here, and you can make the first move."

One by one, Edison's muscles relaxed. He dropped his head and looked back at Caroline. He rotated back around to face her. Just as he had before, he stretched his neck out, touching her with his nose. Once he realized it was still her, he took a few steps toward her.

"Good boy," Caroline muttered under her breath. She put her fingers against his diamond, rubbing in a circular motion again. Edison leaned into her touch.

"Alright, bud, can we put the halter on now? I'll go slow, and I promise I won't hurt you." Caroline made sure to keep one hand on Edison, so she wouldn't startle him. She worked the halter onto his head and fastened the buckle in one motion. Edison lifted his head but stayed calm. She resumed the circles on his forehead.

"Caroline, that was lovely." Jessica set the brush bucket just inside the door. "More than anything I want to stay, but I have a meeting with one of the trainers in the other barn. But I'll be around if you guys need anything, okay?"

"Thanks, Mom. We should be fine." Connor turned his attention back to Caroline as his mom walked away. "How can I help?"

"Do you want to hold him?" Caroline glanced at him over her shoulder.

"Sure, if you think he'll let me."

"We can give it a try. Come on in." Caroline kept rubbing Edison's head as Connor snuck into the stall. Edison eyed him and took a few steps back.

"Caroline, maybe I should stay outside." Connor paused, his hand on the door.

"I think he'll be okay. Try standing right behind me."

Keeping her eyes on Edison, Caroline felt Connor coming closer. Edison watched Connor, the muscles in his shoulder twitching.

"Shhh, you're okay. He's just trying to help you, too." Caroline reached out and rubbed the stallion's shoulder, feeling him relax under her fingers. "Thatta boy."

Connor shifted behind her. "Now what should I do?" he whispered, so close that Caroline could feel his breath on the back of her neck.

Caroline took her hand off Edison's shoulder, turning sideways toward Connor. She reached her hand out to Connor. Her eyes met his. "Here. Put your hand in mine."

Connor blinked. "Really?"

"Really. He needs to see you won't hurt him."

"Alright." Connor reached out, placing his hand in hers.

Caroline felt the heat rise to her cheeks as soon as their fingers touched. She looked down at her boots, forcing herself to breathe. *Come on, focus on the horse. He's what matters here.* She swallowed, turning her eyes back to Edison.

"See, buddy? It's gonna be okay." Caroline lifted their hands up for Edison to sniff. He reached out his neck again, touching them with his nose.

"Okay, Connor. See if you can rub him on his forehead, like I've been doing. Don't move too fast." Caroline sensed Connor nod his head as he lifted his fingers from hers.

Caroline held her breath as Edison held still, letting Connor touch him. He lowered his head, sighing, his eyes closing as he relaxed.

"I can't believe this." Connor smiled at Caroline.

"Me, either. I'll get the brushes." Handing Connor the lead rope, Caroline turned away to reach for the bucket.

Smiling, she felt more like herself than she had in years.

Eighteen

THE NOVEMBER SUN made the small, two-horse trailer feel like summer in the middle of fall. Connor watched as a trickle of sweat slipped down Caroline's forehead, but she didn't move. She didn't flinch to wipe it off. All of her focus was on keeping constant and consistent pressure on the rope in her hand.

They were back in class, working with Luna on loading into the trailer. But all Connor could see was Caroline.

He was still in awe over what she had done with Edison. She had groomed every inch of him, freeing his coat from all the dirt and knots. She had also trimmed his mane, getting rid of all of the tangles.

She had been so confident and so creative with how she introduced Connor to Edison. He'd asked her about it when he walked her to her car at the end of that eventful Saturday.

The sun had started to set. The sky was full of pink and orange streaks. They were later than they had planned to be, as they had gone ahead and done all the painting after she had finished with Edison.

Connor had been sitting on his question all day while they painted, but he could never bring himself to ask her. She had been reaching for her car door when he decided to be brave. "Caroline, can I ask you something?"

Her blue eyes looked up to his, as she nodded her head. "Sure, of course."

"When I came into the stall, with you and Edison, how did you come up with that? You know, putting our hands together, to show him he could trust me?"

Caroline's blushed as she stared down at the ground, scuffing the toe of her boot along the dirt. "Would you believe me if I said I don't know? That it just kind of came to me?"

"I would." Connor took a step toward her to get her to look up at him. "I just wanted to say it was amazing. I wouldn't have thought of it."

Caroline shrugged her shoulders. "Thank you."

"Can I ask something else?" Connor felt his own cheeks turning red.

Caroline laughed. "Sure."

Connor swallowed, looking down. "Maybe this is weird to ask..."

"Connor, what is it?"

"Can I give you a hug? You told my mom you were a hugger, but I've never given you one." Connor's words rushed out of his mouth before he could stop them.

With a smile, Caroline had pushed herself off her car and walked up to him, giving him a hug before he could say anything else.

"There ya go. Now you don't have to ask next time," she had said as they pulled apart, her cheeks just as red as his.

Connor blinked, returning his focus to the present as he heard Luna's hooves step up into the trailer.

"Good girl, Luna. Now, let's get out of here." Connor heard Caroline praise the filly as she backed her out, being sure it was her idea before Luna spooked and left on her own. As always, Caroline's timing and decision-making was perfect.

Caroline's eyes met his as she stepped down from the ramp. Her cheeks were pale, and her forehead looked damp. He took a step toward her. "Do you want me to take her? You could go get a drink?"

"Sure, thank you," she croaked out. Connor held Luna as he watched her walk away.

Lord, thank you for the changes in Caroline. Continue to show me how to help her, to show her how to believe in You again.

He scratched Luna behind her ear. "Alright, little one. Should we go work with the tarp?" Luna sneezed in response.

Connor led the young horse over to the blue tarp that was spread out across the ground. It was one of the hardest obstacles that they would face on their final practical in a couple of weeks. The look of it was enough to get the babies to hesitate, but the noise that it made when they stepped on it was always what frightened them the most.

Connor stopped Luna next to the tarp. She dropped her head, sniffing it. Connor moved his own foot just enough that the toe of his boot touched the edge. It crinkled, causing Luna's ears to flick, but she didn't spook.

"That's my brave girl. Think you can put your hoof on it? Just one?" Connor stepped onto the tarp, putting gentle pressure on the rope. He stayed patient, allowing Luna to think about what she was being asked. Luna lifted her front foot in the air, setting it down on the tarp. Connor gave her a pat on the neck, then turned her away, rewarding her for her effort.

"That was really good," Caroline called out from where she had stopped by the fence.

Connor laughed. "Yeah, right. I have to take what I can get. She doesn't trust me like she trusts you."

Caroline rolled her eyes. "You're crazy."

"Nah, it's the truth. I haven't gotten her in the trailer. No one else in the class has even gotten close to getting their baby in. That's all you."

Caroline tilted her head, looking him right in his eyes. She opened her mouth, but she didn't get a chance to say whatever she was thinking.

"Alright, that's all for today," Dr. Carnes announced. "Let's take them out to the field. Good work, everyone! Have a great Thanksgiving!"

Together, Caroline and Connor led Luna back to the pasture. One by one, the weanlings paraded through the gate. After they had all been set free, they took off at a gallop to the opposite end of the field, celebrating their freedom.

"So, are you still coming over on Friday to work on our final presentation?" Connor double-checked the latch on the gate.

"Yeah, I'll be there." Caroline smiled. "I guess doing homework on Black Friday is better than shopping."

Connor laughed. "I'd have to agree with you there."

"How's Edison?" Caroline asked as they walked back to the barn to get their backpacks.

"He's definitely better. Still skittish around people, but he let me pet him over the door. And he's not pawing or kicking as much. He'll be happy to see you, I'm sure."

Caroline nodded her head. "I'll be happy to see him, too."

The gravel crunched beneath their boots as they walked out to the parking lot together, stopping at the driver's door of Caroline's car.

"Caroline?" Connor asked as he took a step closer.

"Yeah?"

"Have a great Thanksgiving." Connor pulled her into a hug.

"You too, Connor."

He stepped away from her, opening the door. "I'll see you Friday."

"See ya."

Connor headed across the parking lot and climbed into his truck. He called up his driving playlist, hit shuffle, and drove away, looking forward to the long weekend and time with his parents. And another visit from Caroline.

He thought about her all day long while he helped his mom in the kitchen, chopping vegetables and washing dishes, and again when the three of them went outside to give all of the horses a special Thanksgiving treat of carrots and apple slices.

Connor took extra time at Edison's stall, waiting as the stallion finished pulling his treats out of his new bucket. He looked him over, admiring how much better he was looking.

"Caroline sure helped you out, big guy. She'll be here again tomorrow." Connor kept his voice soothing as he spoke. Edison lifted his head from the bucket, chewing his last bite. He looked at Connor, studying him with curious caution. He took a few steps toward him, stopping within reach.

"Hi there," Connor moved his arm from his side, being careful not to startle him. He rested his fingers on Edison's shoulder. The stallion sighed, leaning into Connor's hand.

Connor used his free hand to reach for his phone, an idea popping into his head. He pushed his passcode onto the screen, unlocking it. One more quick tap opened up his camera app. He lifted the phone over the door, snapping a quick picture of his hand against Edison's coat.

Connor stroked the stallion's shoulder once more before stepping back, away from the stall door. A few more quick clicks on the phone, and he was ready to type his message to Caroline.

> 7:32 PM: Happy Thanksgiving!
> Edison and I just wanted to let you
> know we are thankful for you and
> your friendship.

He reread his message, then hit send before he could second-guess himself. He took a deep breath as he stared down at the screen of his phone, watching as the three little dots showed him Caroline was writing back.

> Caroline 7:33 PM: Aww, thank
> you! I am thankful for yours, too.
> Looking forward to seeing you both
> tomorrow :)

Connor smiled as he read her words. He gave all of the stallions one last look before heading down the barn aisle, turning out the light, and stepping into the chilly night air. His smile and Caroline's text kept him warm even though he had left his jacket in the house.

Connor turned around after he climbed the steps to the porch, looking out over the barns, the arenas, and the fields across their property. Even in the dark, with only a few security lights here and there, the view was breathtaking.

Lord, thank You. Thank You for this place, for this life. None of it would be possible without You.

The slightest breeze lifted the leaves of the bushes and the ivy, spreading goosebumps over Connor's arms. It was time to go inside, which meant one thing. One thing that would make it hard for him to sleep.

Tomorrow was almost here.

Nineteen

THE WIND HOWLED and angry raindrops pelted the glass of the windows, but Connor didn't notice. He was too busy working on their final project. Too happy to realize it was storming at all.

They were sitting in their same spots at the kitchen island, perched on their stools as they leaned over their display board, surrounded by colored construction paper and pictures of Luna. Throughout the semester, they had tracked the changes in her weight and height and how she had responded to all of their training. Now it was time to put it all together.

"What if we put the height chart on this side, and the graph showing her changes in weight over here, like this?" Caroline tossed her hair over her shoulder as she set the papers down. "Then we have the rest of the board for the pictures and how she responded to each part of the training."

"Yeah, that looks good to me. Honestly, whatever you want to do is fine. You can design, and I'll glue it down." Connor twirled the glue stick around in his hand as he smiled at her.

Caroline laughed. "Fair enough. Just make sure to center it on the construction paper, before you put it down on the board."

"You got it." Connor saluted her as he moved closer to start gluing. Caroline rolled her eyes as she reached for the scissors.

Connor watched her from the corner of his eye as she studied the photos they had taken of each other working with Luna, showing all of the different things they had done with her through the semester. Caroline was careful to select the right color of paper for each picture. He was impressed as she matched an item from each picture, like one of their shirts or Luna's halter, with construction paper the same color, and then laid each one out in a staggered pattern. Each picture popped against its background.

"You're good at this." Connor pointed at the board.

"Thanks. I used to do a lot of scrapbooking, and this kind of feels like that."

"Used to? How come not anymore?"

Caroline adjusted the last picture onto the board. "I guess I'm not doing anything worth scrapbooking these days."

"What do you mean?"

"Like softball and uh...just stuff like that. I've kinda lost everything that I used to get pictures of." Caroline shrugged her shoulders.

Connor nodded his head, feeling the weight of her words, and of the ones she left unsaid. "Maybe you could make one for this semester. You already have all the pictures."

Caroline tilted her head as she studied their display, blinking a few times as she took it all in. "Yeah, maybe."

They were quiet for a few minutes as Connor finished gluing everything down. He kept glancing at her, wondering if it was time he let her know he knew about her accident. To let her know she didn't have to hide that part of her past.

He stood the board up on the island. They both stepped back across the kitchen, so they could see it from a distance.

"I'd say it looks pretty good," Caroline said first. "What do you think?" She turned her head to the side to look at him.

"I'd say it looks great. Thanks to you." Connor nudged her with his elbow.

Caroline smiled as she nudged him back. "Not just me. We did it together."

Connor nodded his head, his mind made up that they were close enough friends now that he could ask her about her accident, and what had brought her back to horses after so much time. He walked back to his stool at the island and swallowed a drink of water from his glass.

"Can I ask you something?" He turned to see she had followed him.

She gave him a sideways smile. "You don't always have to ask me if you can ask me something. It's okay to just ask."

Connor felt heat in his cheeks. "Alright. I'm sorry. I guess I do that a lot."

"No need to be sorry. I just thought I'd let you know you can ask me whatever you want to."

Connor nodded his head, pressing his lips together as he tried to figure out how to word what he wanted to say. He cleared his throat and looked into her eyes. "Caroline, I..." As he opened his mouth and started to speak, the front door crashed opened, bringing in the sounds of the wind and rain. They both jumped.

"Connor? Are you around?" Connor's dad called out from the entryway.

Connor tore his eyes away from Caroline's and stood up from his stool. "In the kitchen, Dad."

Greg came around the corner, his black windbreaker jacket dripping from the rain. "I hate to bug you, but do you think you could help us out in the barn? We're trying to get everybody fed and that stallion is all worked up because of the weather."

"Edison?" Caroline asked, her eyes growing wide.

Greg nodded his head. "I'm afraid he's going to hurt himself or somebody."

"I'll come help." She started to head for the front door.

Connor followed her. "Caroline, are you sure? Don't you need to get home?"

"That was the other thing I needed to tell you." Greg interrupted before Caroline could answer. "The wind knocked a huge tree down on the highway. It's closed both ways. I think she's stuck here for a while."

"I'll call my parents and let them know after we get Edison settled. Let's go." Caroline pulled her sweatshirt over her head, and then whipped her hair up into a ponytail.

"Here, let me get you something a little more waterproof." Connor headed down the hall to the closet.

"I better get back to your mom, Connor. I'll see you guys out there." Greg turned and headed out the door.

"We'll be right behind you." Connor came back with two windbreakers in his hand,

"Thank you." Caroline reached for the doorknob.

"You're welcome." Connor caught her hand before she could go outside. "You know you don't have to do this, right?"

Caroline stared down at their hands, then looked up to meet his eyes. "I know, but he needs help. And I know you'll be with me." Caroline squeezed his hand.

Connor swallowed, doing his best to ignore everything he was feeling from that squeeze. He blinked once. "Yes, I will. Let's go."

They pushed the door open and stepped onto the porch. They both ran down the steps, fighting the wind as it blew them sideways.

"How did we not realize it had gotten this bad?" Caroline screamed so Connor could hear her.

"I guess we were really focused on our presentation." Connor yelled back, wiping the sting of the rain away from his eyes. *God, please help us calm Edison down and get the other horses taken care of. And keep Caroline safe. Please let the storm stop soon,* Connor prayed as they continued to run.

They reached the doorway of the stallion barn and ducked inside. Jessica and Greg stood in front of Edison's stall, talking to him, trying to get him to calm down. But the stallion was snorting and squealing, kicking at the walls. Caroline sprinted ahead of Connor.

"Hey, bud," Caroline whispered as Connor came up behind her. "It's okay, it's just the storm. No one here is going to hurt you."

Edison froze at the sound of her voice, his muscles rigid, ready to explode at any moment. He whinnied, loud and high-pitched, desperate for comfort.

Connor held his breath as Caroline reached for the latch of the stall door. She squeaked it open, letting herself inside. Edison whinnied again, dropping his head down to her.

She reached his shoulder, rubbing him with her knuckles. Edison sighed, relaxing under her touch. He turned his head toward her, resting his nose in her hair.

"That's amazing." Greg took a step forward to the stall door. "You have a God-given gift there, young lady."

Connor watched Caroline's eyes fall at the mention of God, but she gave his dad a polite smile. "I'm not sure about that, but thank you."

"Well, I'm sure. I'm completely sure." Greg ran a hand through his wet hair. "I guess we ought to get everyone else fed."

Connor looked at his dad. "I can help you."

Jessica stepped forward and put a hand on Connor's shoulder. "We got it, kiddo. You can stay here with Caroline."

Connor opened his mouth to argue, but as he looked at Caroline in the stall with Edison, he knew he didn't want to leave her. "Alright. But please, let me know if you guys need anything."

Jessica smiled at him. "We will, and you guys do the same."

Connor watched as Caroline ran her fingers through Edison's forelock. He could see her mouth moving but couldn't hear anything she was saying. He leaned into the stall door, in awe as the stallion was already as calm as he had been with her the other day. She did have a gift. A gift that she had given up on because of fear. A gift he wanted to help her rediscover.

God, help me here. Give me the right words to talk to her.

"Caroline, can I...?" Connor stopped, and cleared his throat.

Caroline looked over her shoulder at him. "Can you ask me something?" She grinned as she teased him.

"Well...yeah. Sorry. Old habits are hard to break."

She laughed. "No worries. Do you want to come in here? Maybe hand me his grain bucket, see if he'll eat?"

Connor nodded as he came into the stall. He grabbed the bucket and stepped over to Caroline and Edison. The stallion perked his ears, looking at the bucket with interest.

Caroline took it from Connor and cradled it in her arms. "Hungry, big guy? You can eat."

Edison put his head down and began chewing on his dinner. Caroline looked up at Connor, her eyes the happiest he had ever seen. "So, what did you want to ask me?"

Connor reached over and patted Edison on the neck. "Remember when we had lunch in the union? You told me you used to believe in God, but you didn't want to explain it then. Do you think you could now?"

Caroline looked away from him, her eyes falling to Edison's ears. Connor watched her blink as she bit her lip. He took a step closer to her.

"I'm sorry. You don't have to." Connor put his hand on her arm.

She looked up at him again as she felt his touch. "No, it's okay. It's pretty simple."

"Simple?"

"Yeah." Caroline shrugged her shoulders. "I've had to deal with too much pain and loss to keep believing He cares about me or my future."

"I can understand that. Completely." Connor swallowed.

"You can?" Caroline wrinkled her forehead as she looked at him.

"Yeah, I can." He had asked God to give him the right words to say to her so many times over the last few months. And now, he knew what he had to do. He had to tell Caroline about Emily.

Twenty

THE WIND HAD EASED UP, but the rain was still coming down hard, bouncing off the roof and sides of the barn. Edison was munching on his hay, as quiet as the other stallions. Caroline leaned back against the stall door, waiting for Connor to come back from the house with their dinner.

They had checked the traffic reports and discovered that the highway would be closed overnight. She had already called her parents and explained to them that she wouldn't be home until tomorrow. Even though Edison was settled, she wasn't ready to leave the barn, so Connor had offered to go get them something to eat.

Caroline knew Connor had something he wanted to tell her. His demeanor had changed ever since she told him why she didn't believe in God anymore, and she had never seen his eyes look so sad.

Whatever it was, she hoped she could handle it.

Connor ducked in the barn door at the end of the aisle, a plastic shopping bag draped over one arm. He flipped the hood of his jacket off his head with his free hand as he walked toward her.

"Well, I did my best to keep everything dry. But I'm not sure how well I did." Connor smiled at her, but it didn't reach his eyes.

"I'm sure it'll be fine. I don't think you could keep anything dry out there."

"That's for sure. I hope grilled ham and cheese sandwiches are okay? My mom thought we should eat something warm."

"Sounds great." Caroline took the sandwich wrapped in tin foil that Connor handed her, enjoying the warmth on her fingers.

"I should've brought us a couple of chairs." Connor looked up and down the aisle, searching for something they could sit on. He handed the bag to Caroline and disappeared into the feed room.

Caroline's mouth popped open as he reappeared, carrying a large bale of hay. "Connor, I would have helped you carry that."

"It's all good, I got it." He sat it down in front of Edison's stall. He swung the door open, then scooted the hay bale in front of the opening. "There ya go, a front row seat."

"Thank you." Caroline sat down on one end of the bale, resting her back against the door frame. Connor sat down on the other end, placing the bag in the middle.

"You're welcome. There are some chips and bottles of water in there, too."

They ate in silence, enjoying the warm and gooey cheese. Finishing first, Connor crumbled up his tin foil, putting it into the now-empty bag. He took a drink from his water bottle, then met Caroline's eyes.

He coughed, clearing his throat. "Do you remember Dream? From the first time you were here?"

Caroline nodded. "Your sister's jumper. She's in the broodmare barn."

"You got it." Connor lifted his lips into a small smile. "Do you remember anything else?" Caroline thought back.

"Yeah, I think so. You told me she was jumping about four feet and could have done more, but plans changed."

"Right again." Connor dropped his eyes to the bale of hay, pulling on a few stems. Caroline thought she heard him sniff.

"Can I ask what changed?" Caroline whispered, not wanting to force him to tell her.

Connor pressed his lips together and nodded his head. When his eyes met Caroline's, she could see the tears. "My sister, Emily. She was killed in a car accident two years ago."

Caroline felt the shock fill her expression. "Connor, I am so sorry. I had no idea."

"It's okay. I don't talk about her much." Connor shrugged his shoulders. "Is it okay if I tell you the whole story? Now that I've brought it up?"

"Yes, of course." Caroline crossed her arms over her chest, fighting off the damp chill that was beginning to hang in the air.

Connor leaned back, settling against the door frame opposite from Caroline, so that they were facing each other. "I guess I should start by saying I idolized my big sister. I was that kid, you know, the 'annoying little brother,' but Emily never got tired of me. We were best friends."

"How far apart in age were you?" Caroline kept her voice quiet.

"Four years, but it didn't really matter."

Connor looked up at her, pain showing in his expression. Caroline tried to smile, hoping it would comfort him.

"Anyway, Emily got Dream when she was sixteen, and Dream was five. It's hard to believe it now, but she was almost as wild and crazy as this one here." Connor tilted his head toward Edison.

"Really? Had she been abused?"

"We don't know for sure. My parents picked her up at an auction and didn't get any information on her, except that she was a Thoroughbred. They couldn't even load her into the trailer. They had to back it up to her pen and chase her in. They had to unload her the same way, too."

"Emily wasn't afraid of her?"

Connor chuckled. "No, she was fearless. Always had been. She went right into that pen, and had that mare settled down and bonded with her in less than an hour. She had a gift. A lot like you. You remind me of her."

Caroline blushed. *Or of the me I used to be.* She sniffed and stared down at her hands. "I don't think so. She sounds pretty amazing."

"She was. It didn't take her long to train Dream. She did it all practically by herself. They started competing and won just about everything. They had their sights set on Grand Prix."

"It sounds like they would have made it."

"They would have. They each had individual talent, but their bond is what made them special. Emily hardly had to give her any kind of cues. They just read each other's minds and hearts. It was incredible to watch."

Caroline felt the familiar break in her own heart cracking open. She looked over to Edison, keeping her eyes hidden. Connor continued talking, either ignoring her tears, or not seeing them.

"Emily had signed up for a clinic in Tucson with one of the best jumper riders in the country. Dream had a minor abscess in her hoof, so she couldn't take her. But Emily still went to watch. Even though she couldn't ride, she wanted to learn everything she could. We were all going to go, but since she wasn't taking Dream, she just drove herself in her car, and we stayed home."

Caroline looked back at him as she heard Connor sniff. He wiped one single tear from his cheek, then made eye contact with her.

"It happened on her way home that night. She was already off the interstate, and on the highway coming here. An oncoming car swerved to avoid a deer, and lost control, veering into her lane. They hit her head on."

Caroline stood and closed the distance between them. She sat down next to him on the hay bale and pulled him into a hug. "I'm so sorry, Connor."

Their hug ended, but Connor kept ahold of her hand. "Thank you." He attempted to smile. "It was hard for a long time. I felt guilty for not going with her. I thought if I had been there, we could have avoided the crash, or I could've done something to save her. I was angry at God for taking her from us, for not letting her or Dream live out what so easily could have been their legacy."

Caroline was hanging on his every word as he described everything she had felt since her accident. "How did you get past it? The guilt? The anger?"

"Some days are easier than others, for sure. But it all came down to one verse I found in the Bible. Romans 8:28. 'And we know that in all things God works for the good of those who love Him, who have been called according to His purpose.'"

Caroline focused on her boots, not sure of what to say. Connor squeezed her hand.

"I don't understand the way God works. I don't understand why Emily is gone. But I know He loves me and has a plan for me. Not just for me, but for every one of us. Even in our tragedies and pain, He has a plan and He always cares. And like I said, it's easier some days to believe that than others."

Caroline nodded, too overwhelmed by her thoughts to speak. She felt tears in her eyes, but she looked up at Connor anyway. "Thank you, for telling me all of this. I'm sure it wasn't easy."

"You're welcome, Caroline. I haven't told anyone any of that before, but I thought you needed to hear it. So thank you for listening." Connor pulled her into another hug. "I just want you to know, there still is a plan for you and He does still care. Even through all of the loss."

Caroline couldn't say anything because of the tears that closed in on her throat, but she nodded her head into his shoulder. When they pulled apart, Connor looked at his watch.

"It's getting late. And cold. We might want to head inside."

Caroline looked at Edison. "Do you think he'll be okay?"

Connor stood and went to the nearest window. "It's finally stopped raining, so I think he'll stay quiet. We can always come back if it starts up again."

"Alright." Caroline got up and went to Edison, running her fingers through his blond mane. "Goodnight, buddy. Get some rest." Edison lifted his head from his hay and breathed in Caroline's ear.

Leaving the stall, Connor and Caroline pushed the hay bale to the side so they could shut the door. They walked to the house, their arms brushing as they went, and climbed up the steps to the porch. Connor stopped and turned back, looking out toward the barns. The paths were lit with lanterns, causing the stones to glisten from the rain.

"What's wrong?" Caroline followed his gaze, trying to see or hear whatever had stopped him.

"Nothing is wrong. I do this every night. Look out over everything and remember how blessed I am to live this life. This, right here, is my favorite view."

Caroline looked out again, this time not looking for something wrong, but appreciating it for what it was. "It is beautiful."

"Caroline, is it okay if I pray?"

She studied him and saw the sadness still clinging to his eyes. If praying was what he needed to do, she wouldn't get in his way. "Sure."

Connor took her hand before he closed his eyes and began. "Lord, thank you for this day and for keeping us safe. Thank you that Caroline was here to calm Edison down, and thank you for her friendship. I haven't been able to talk about Emily in a long time, and I needed to. Please help us remember You have a purpose for us, even through all of the pain and loss that we can't understand. In Your name I pray, Amen."

Connor opened his eyes and looked at her. "Thank you."

"You're welcome. For what it's worth, I'm glad I was here tonight."

Connor smiled as he let her in the front door of the house. All of the lights were off, except for one in the kitchen, and one over the stairs. "My mom left you some clothes on the bed in the guest room," Connor told her as they headed up. "If you need anything else, I'm right across the hall."

"Okay, thank you."

"You're welcome. Goodnight, Caroline."

"Goodnight, Connor."

Inside the guest room, Caroline fingered the clothes on the bed, then padded across the carpet to the window. The room was right above the porch, so she had the same view Connor had just told her was his favorite.

She stood there, staring out of the damp glass, replaying everything he had told her. He was right, he did understand why she didn't believe anymore. He understood more about her than she had ever thought someone could. Maybe one day she would be able to tell him the truth, tell him her own story.

And maybe one day, he'd be able to help her believe again.

Twenty-One

THE SUNLIGHT DANCING THROUGH THE LEAVES of the trees erased every reminder of the storm that had rattled the barns two days before. All the rain and wind had left behind was the clean, crisp smell of autumn. Caroline was back at Connor's, helping him and his parents finish the last-minute details before their open house started.

Caroline sneaked away from the breeding barn, where everything would take place, to spend just a few minutes with Edison. She was grateful that guests to the open house would be kept out of the stallion barn. The chestnut horse was doing well, but Caroline didn't want strangers roaming through and upsetting him.

Her footsteps echoed down the aisle as she headed for his stall. She reached into her back pocket and pulled out the carrot she had grabbed for him from the bucket on one of the tables. Edison popped his head over the stall door, nickering at her and bobbing his head.

"Hi, big guy. How's it going? You think this is for you?" Caroline snapped the carrot in half, leaving her palm flat as Edison pulled it into his mouth. He crunched away, then reached for the rest of it. "Alright, alright, there ya go, bud."

"How did I know I'd find you in here?" Connor called as he walked down the aisle.

"Probably because I'm predictable. I'm sorry. I just

wanted to see him before everything got started out there."

"So, you weren't planning on hiding out in here the whole time?" Connor grinned as he stopped beside her.

"Well...I won't lie, the thought did occur to me. But only because I don't want anyone to scare him." Caroline gave Connor her best innocent smile.

"Ahh, I see. I promise he'll be okay. We won't let anyone in. We have a book in the barn with all of the stallion information, pictures, and pedigrees. If someone really wants to see one, my dad will come get him, and show him outside the barn. And if anyone asks for Edison, we're just going to say he's not available today, which people should understand, considering everything he's been through."

Caroline gave Edison one last look. "Alright. I'll see you later then, buddy."

"Come on, people are starting to show up. We should get some food before all of the good stuff is gone." They walked side by side back to the breeding barn, their elbows brushing every few steps.

Connor handed Caroline a plate as they got in line. She grabbed a few pieces of fruit, cheese, and crackers, and followed him to Dream's stall.

Caroline's affection had grown for the mare since Connor had told her everything. She put one hand on the mare's long blaze. She could imagine that the pain of losing your owner, your person, had to mirror everything she felt in losing Beau.

"What are you thinking about?" Connor asked her in between bites. "You looked pretty deep in thought there."

Caroline swallowed, not looking away from Dream as she answered. "Just that it had to be hard on her, too, losing Emily."

Connor put his hand over Caroline's. "It was. It took

her a long time to get over it. And there are days I think she still misses her."

"I'm sure she does, too." Caroline met Connor's eyes, seeing that his emotions matched her own. *He would understand you. You should just tell him.* She licked her lips. "Connor, I'm...I'm—"

"Hey, Connor! I was hoping I'd run into you. How's school going?" A tall gentleman wearing a large cowboy hat interrupted her. Caroline closed her mouth.

She could tell Connor wanted to know what she was going to say, but he tore his gaze away from her. "Mr. Erickson, it's good to see you. School is going great. I'm really enjoying the equine program."

"I knew you would. You are your father's son. Now, listen. I was talking with your dad a few weeks back, and he told me you guys have a mare in foal to Southern Comfort. I love that stallion and all his progeny. Is she in this barn? Could you show her to me?"

Connor glanced at Caroline, so she nodded her head. "I'll wait here. You go ahead."

"Thank you." Connor turned back to Mr. Erickson. "Sure thing. She's right down here. I can show you her pedigree, too, if you'd like."

Caroline smiled as she listened to Connor talk about everything he knew about the mare, the stallion, and what the foal should be like based on the crossing. He had found his purpose, the plan for his life. Even after all he'd been through.

Maybe there was still hope for her.

"Caroline? Caroline Davis?" A female voice spoke from beside her. Caroline turned, and all of the blood drained from her face.

"It is you! Honey, how are you? I didn't realize you had

started riding again! Is your mom here, too?" The woman pulled Caroline into a hug. Caroline went through the motions to hug her back.

"Hi, Mrs. Richardson," Caroline muttered into the shoulder of one of her mother's longtime clients. "No, Mom isn't here."

Mrs. Richardson released her from the hug, making eye contact. "What brings you here, then?"

Caroline gulped. "I'm, um, a friend of Connor Taylor's. He invited me."

"Oh, how wonderful! I hear he's a lovely young man. You'll have to introduce me to him. I have a few horses I want to see, but we'll have to catch up later, okay? I'll be sure to find you." She waved at Caroline as she walked away.

Caroline felt cold, clammy sweat beading at the back of her neck. She looked around the barn, searching for the bathroom. She found the sign, right next to the feed room.

Flipping on the light, she locked the door behind her. She grabbed a paper towel, wetting it with cold water from the sink. Placing it on the back of her neck, she closed her eyes and forced herself to breathe.

You should have considered the possibility someone would recognize you. Why are you even here?

Two faces appeared in her head as she asked herself that question. Edison. And Connor.

Edison needed her. And she was beginning to admit to herself, she needed him, too. He was helping her find her way back.

And Connor. He knew pain and how to overcome it. He had found a purpose. She needed him to show her how.

They were the reasons she was here.

Connor. She needed to find him, and she needed to tell

him everything before Mrs. Richardson did.

Caroline threw away the paper towel, unlocked the door, and stepped back into the barn aisle. She looked through the crowd but couldn't find him anywhere. Reaching for her phone, she realized a quick text would be her best option.

> 12:54 PM: Can you meet me at
> Edison's stall? There's something I
> need to tell you.

As she hit send, hoof beats pounded outside the barn. Everyone crowded into the doorway, straining to see the loose horse.

Caroline followed, thinking this would be her moment to get to the stallion barn unseen. But when the flash of red streaked by the door, panic filled her stomach.

She pushed her way past everyone to the front of the crowd, confirming for herself that Edison was the loose horse. Connor, his dad, and a few stable hands were already at work trying to catch him.

He was beautiful. He moved with beauty and grace; his tail arched over his back as he avoided the men with ease.

Edison paused for a moment, letting Connor get closer. He had a halter in his hand, and Caroline watched as he approached him like she had that first day, extending his arm out, letting Edison smell him. But Edison wasn't ready.

He spun away from Connor, leaping in the air and kicking out, missing Connor by inches, sending him to the ground. Caroline ran from the barn, heading for Connor, but Edison saw her first.

He whinnied, galloping straight for her. Caroline froze, fearing that he was going too fast to stop, thinking he would run her over for sure. She lifted her hands out to her side, hoping that would help. "Whoa," she breathed.

Edison skidded to a stop in front of her. Caroline kept her eyes down, and her voice low, as she stepped to the side, approaching his shoulder. "Easy, bud. Just relax. No one is going to hurt you."

Caroline stretched out her arm and rubbed him with her knuckles, as she had before. Edison twitched and arched his neck, but he didn't run. "Thatta boy. Just stay with me here, okay?"

Connor walked up behind her. "Caroline, here, you better put it on him. I don't think he'll let me."

Caroline reached behind with her free hand, opening her palm for the halter. When she felt the leather in her hand, she closed her fingers around it. She pulled it around in front of her. Edison snorted.

"Hey now, it's okay. It's just me. We're gonna put this on you and get you back to your stall." Edison looked at her sideways as she guided the halter onto his head, buckling it by his ear. She took a step back and started to walk him toward his barn.

Edison tossed his head in protest to the pressure on the lead rope. Caroline looked up at his eyes and saw a familiar expression. Anger and panic filled his face and he jerked, pulling at the rope in her hand, trying to regain his freedom. He reared, pawing at the air. The sudden movement knocked her off her feet.

"Edison, whoa!" Caroline gripped at the rope as she struggled to get up. She managed to stand as Edison landed and put her hand on his neck to calm him down, to keep him from going up again.

"Caroline, are you okay?" Connor put his hand on her shoulder.

Her throat was closing, and no audible words came out of her mouth. Dark circles closed in around her, impairing her sight. She tried to blink them away, but a picture from her past flooded her vision.

The horse's emotions were the same, but he was gray instead of red. He was lying on his side, thrashing and screaming as he tried to get up. Caroline was on the ground next to him, struggling to get up herself, but she couldn't. His weight on her legs was too great, and her left foot was caught in the stirrup underneath him. She tried to soothe him, but their pain had been too extreme.

"Caroline?" Connor stepped to the side of her, the memory dissipating as he came into her sight. "What's wrong?"

"Let's just get him back to the barn," Caroline whispered as she started to walk, being careful not to put any pressure on the rope this time. Edison followed her, still on edge, but his eyes were quieter.

Connor stayed at her elbow, one eye on her and one eye on Edison as they walked him to the barn. Murmurs echoed through the crowd, but the onlookers stayed quiet and respected their space. The stallion behaved, but Caroline didn't try to take a breath until she was on the other side of his stall door.

Even then she still couldn't breathe. She began gasping for air, grasping Connor's hand as she tried to keep from collapsing.

"What is it? What's wrong? Are you hurt?" Connor held onto her hand.

Caroline could only shake her head, communicating she couldn't speak, as she bent forward at the waist. Connor put his other hand on her back, trying to help her relax.

Caroline wasn't sure how much time passed before she was able to draw a full breath. Straightening, she looked at Connor, tears falling from her eyes. "I...I should go."

Connor squeezed her fingers. "No, please, wait. Talk to me. What's wrong?"

Caroline hesitated, looking into his eyes, her heart breaking as she longed to tell him everything. "Connor... I'm sorry. I can't. I just, can't."

Tears poured down her face as she ran as fast as she could to her car, not looking back as she ignored Edison's confused whinnies.

And the pleading sound of Connor calling her name.

Twenty-Two

CONNOR FELT HELPLESS AS HE WATCHED Caroline's trembling hands and looked into her fearful eyes and flushed face. She had struggled to take notes during the lecture, and she was doing as little as possible with Luna. It was obvious to him she was back—the Caroline from the beginning of the semester.

And more than anything, he wanted to know why.

She had come so far, and maybe he had been imagining it, but she had started to bond and build a relationship with Edison.

And with him.

Connor ran his hand through his hair, watching as Caroline tried to back Luna through the L-shaped poles. Just the other day, she had done it without making a mistake. But today, Luna was confused by her shaking. She was trying to understand, but Caroline's signals weren't clear. She kept stepping over the pole.

"Can I help?" Connor pushed away from the fence.

Caroline's eyes snapped up to his, but just for a moment. "Do you want to just take her?"

"No, you're doing okay. She's trying really hard to do what you want."

"Connor, please?" Her eyes held tears as she asked.

His heart softened at her sadness. "Will you try one more time? For me? I'll be right here."

Caroline bit her lip but nodded her head.

At least she still trusts me, Connor thought to himself as he stepped right behind Caroline. "I'm going to put my hand over yours on the lead rope. You guide her, but I'll just be here to help steady her, okay? Kind of like what we did with Edison."

Caroline gasped at the sound of the stallion's name, but she didn't object as Connor reached for her hand. Together, they were able to back Luna through the poles. The filly sighed in relief as she cleared the last one.

"Alright, guys, that's a wrap for today. Let's take them back to the field." Dr. Carnes called out before heading for the gate.

"Now will you take her?" Caroline whispered, her knuckles white.

"Yeah, but will you wait for me? In the parking lot?"

Caroline looked into his eyes. "Yeah, I will."

"Thank you."

She nodded her head, turning and heading for the classroom. Connor got in line, joining the parade of weanlings heading for the pasture.

He gave Luna a few extra scratches on her neck as he took off her halter. "Thank you for being so good." Luna licked her lips before trotting away to join her friends.

Connor swung the halter over his shoulder, sighing as he latched the gate to the field. He took his time walking back to the barn, gathering his thoughts as he put the halter away and grabbed his backpack. As his eyes lifted to the parking lot, he found Caroline sitting on the tailgate of his truck, her arms folded across her midsection as she stared down at her knees.

God, she looks so sad. Please, make her want to talk to me. Help me say the right words.

Connor tossed his backpack in the passenger seat of his truck, then went around and sat down next to Caroline. He looked at her, waiting for her to say something, anything, but she continued to stare down.

"What did you want to tell me?"

Caroline lifted her chin, confusion wrinkling her eyebrows. "What do you mean?"

"Yesterday. Before Edison got out. You had sent me a text asking me to meet you at his stall because you needed to tell me something."

"Oh." Caroline blinked. She swallowed, pressing her lips together. "I guess it doesn't really matter anymore."

Connor strained to hear her whispered words. "I'm sure it does. Caroline, please talk to me."

"Connor, I can't. I can't do this." She jumped down, swinging her bag over her shoulder and taking a few steps toward her car.

"What can't you do?" Connor gripped the edge of the tailgate, forcing himself not to run after her.

"Whatever this is." Her hands gestured between the two of them as she turned back to face him. "Or horses. I just can't do it. I'll try to finish the semester, but that's it."

Connor let the silence settle between them. He tilted his head, studying her. Her eyes found his, and the pain he saw there was more than he could take. He slid down and walked to her.

"Caroline...I know about you, and your accident." He kept his eyes and his voice soft and kind as he spoke.

All of the color drained from Caroline's face. "Mrs. Richardson found you?"

"Who?" Connor reached for her hand.

"Mrs. Richardson. She was at the open house. She recognized me. That's why I texted you. I didn't want her to tell you before I could. But you didn't talk to her?"

"No, she didn't tell me anything. I don't even know who she is."

Caroline studied him, her eyes growing wet. "Then how do you know?"

Connor took a breath, running his thumb across the top of her hand before answering. "I recognized you, on the first day of class. Our parents have done business together off and on over the years. I've seen you ride, and I've seen you compete. I knew who you were the moment you walked in."

Tears spilled out onto her cheeks. "But you never said anything."

"You looked so scared, and I'd heard you'd given up on horses. I was so surprised to see you here, and then you told Dr. Carnes you didn't have any horse experience at all. I figured you didn't want anyone to know." Connor shrugged his shoulders.

Caroline looked down at her boots. "No, I didn't. It wasn't until yesterday that I even wanted to tell you."

"I know. But why did you say that it doesn't matter anymore?"

Caroline sniffed, wiping away a few tears on her cheek. "Because I can't do this, Connor. I'm not like you. I can't move past it or believe again. It hurts too much."

"But you could be like me. You could believe again. Just let me help you." Connor felt like he was begging.

"Why do you care so much?"

Connor fought away the pain that was taking over in his heart. "I couldn't save Emily. Or even help her. It was all out of my control. But I can help you."

Fresh tears welled in Caroline's eyes. "Connor..." Her voice was overtaken by sobs.

Connor pulled her into a hug, tears now stinging his own eyes. "Please, Caroline. Let me be here for you."

Caroline sniffed, then pulled herself out of his arms. "Please, just let me go. The girl you're trying to help...she doesn't exist anymore. I can't be her."

Connor didn't reach for her as she jogged to her car. He let her go, as she had asked. But as she opened her door, he had to ask one last question. "Then who are you?"

Caroline hesitated, blinking several times as she considered his question. She shrugged her shoulders. "I don't know."

Before Connor could respond, she ducked into her seat, slammed the door, and drove away. All he could do was stare at the dust her tires kicked up and pray that she would be okay.

And wonder how he'd ever be able to let her go.

Twenty-Three

THE COLD BREEZE LIFTED HER BLOND HAIR, blowing it around her cheeks, the ends sticking to her face because of her tears. Caroline pulled her royal-blue sweatshirt closer to her body, setting the hood over her head, and folding the ends of the sleeves over her hands. She leaned back onto the cold metal of the top rail of the bleachers, crossing her arms over her chest and resting her feet on the seat in front of her.

The crowd was thin, so it had been easy to find a seat alone. That was the story of her life now. Alone.

She wasn't sure why she was here. But between the bad dreams and the loneliness, she had needed to get out of her house.

All of her finals were done. All of her grades for the semester were set. There was no homework to distract her, and no friends to occupy her time. She had made sure of that when she cut off all communication with anyone who had ever cared about her.

Caroline's bad dreams alternated between softball and horses. She would be on the mound, throwing her last pitch. Then the pain would shoot down her arm as the ground opened up and swallowed her whole, sending her tumbling into the darkness.

But the horse dreams were worse. She was always trapped, always in pain, always unable to breathe, and suffocated by fear and pain—hers and the horse's. The horse kept switching, changing between gray and red. Between Beau and Edison.

This particular evening, tired of staring at the walls, dreading another night of nightmares, she had gotten in her car and left. She had driven around until she saw the lights sparkling against the night sky. The lights drew her in, and she found herself in the parking lot of the ballpark she had spent endless hours at during her little league and ponytail years.

And she was learning that maybe softball hurt less than horses after all.

Caroline had been debating returning to the softball team, resuming her position as manager, after Christmas break. She could find a degree that would help her get into coaching. Sure, it wouldn't be the same as playing, but it would be something...even though watching was making her cry. It would be a purpose for her life.

She could still use her knowledge to help the team get outs. Maybe she wasn't the one throwing the pitches to home plate, but she could call them. She could study scouting reports and films of opposing hitters and decide what pitches would work best against them. She'd been doing it tonight, while she watched the game.

From her guess, the girls playing were thirteen or fourteen. Old enough to be competitive, but young enough to still be carefree and enjoy the game. The pitchers for both teams were pretty good. They could hit their spots and change speeds, and they had good spin on their pitches.

Caroline wouldn't say she was enjoying herself, but the game was a good distraction. It was keeping her from thinking about Connor and the pain she knew she had caused him. She felt awful about it, but better for it to end now than later down the road. He would be okay. He knew what he was going to do with his life.

But that didn't stop her from missing him.

He had been good to her all semester, helping her overcome her fears and helping her get through the class. He'd become her friend, sharing things with her that he wouldn't tell just anyone, showing her he could relate to the pain and loss she'd experienced in her life.

He had even kept her secret.

Caroline ran her hand through her bangs, refocusing on the game, as it was down to the last out. The team batting was down by a run but had a runner on second base. As the next batter stepped up, the cheers of the hitting team grew louder. She was one of the tallest girls on the field, and from the excitement her teammates were expressing in the dugout, she was one of the best hitters, too.

The pitcher walked to the back of the circle and took a deep breath as she faced center field. Caroline smiled through her tears at the routine that was so much like hers had been. That small pause always had given her a moment to clear her head and focus on the next pitch, no matter what had happened with the previous one.

Caroline looked on as the pitcher delivered the pitch. Changeup inside. The hitter watched it meet the catcher's glove, taking it for strike one. *Good job.*

Watching the hitter take a few swings as the pitcher prepared for the next pitch, Caroline thought about what she would throw next. *Something hard and fast, outside corner.*

She focused on the pitcher's wrist, trying to see what she was throwing. Her fingers and palm stayed behind the ball, her snap coming straight through. A fastball.

Caroline could tell it was headed for the outside part of the plate. The batter swung, fouling it straight back into the backstop. The changeup had done its job, messing with the hitter's timing just enough for her to miss the next pitch.

Drop ball, inside. Way inside, for a ball. Make her chase it. She encouraged the young pitcher in her head, telling her the same things she had told herself time and time again.

Again, Caroline zeroed in on the girl's hand, identifying the pitch as she threw it. Caroline held her breath as she saw her snap her hand over the top of the ball, pointing her index finger down toward the ground, creating the drop ball spin. But her release had been too far out in front of her hip. The ball wouldn't have time to drop.

Sure enough, the ball stayed up. The batter made strong contact, sending it into the night sky toward center field. The girls in the dugout erupted with screams; the pitcher put her glove over her mouth, frozen as she waited. The center fielder had just enough room to make the catch, one hand against the fence as she reached for the ball, securing it in her glove for the out.

Caroline felt the pitcher's relief as she watched the girl jump up and down before running to give her outfielder a hug. She knew that feeling of victory well. But she also felt the disappointment of the hitter. The pain of having been so close, but to come up short.

There were two sides to every win. Two stories for each loss.

Caroline sighed, glancing at the time on her Fitbit. 7:04. It was early enough that she wasn't ready to go home, but late enough that she wasn't sure what to do, besides go back to driving around.

She climbed down from the bleachers, sticking her arms in the pouch of her sweatshirt. Head down, she started the walk back to her car.

"Caroline?" a voice called out.

She turned and looked, worried about who could have recognized her here, after the incident at the open house. A blond head and green eyes peered out from the window of the concessions stand. "Ryan?"

"What are you doing here?" Ryan stepped outside.

"I could ask you the same thing." Caroline tilted her head as he walked over to her.

"Just doing some volunteering." Ryan laughed. "What about you?"

"I was just driving around and saw the lights. I guess they kinda drew me in."

Ryan nodded his head. "So, how have you been?"

Caroline watched his eyes, seeing if he was being sincere. "I've been okay. What about you?"

"I've been okay too." He hesitated, looking down at the ground before making eye contact again. "What are you up to, now that the game is over?"

"Um..." Caroline bit her lip. "I'm really not sure."

"Would you want to head over to campus, maybe get something to eat? We could catch up a little. No pressure though. Just a thought."

Caroline looked at him, not sure of what to say. Maybe she had been too quick to end things. Maybe she should have talked to him, given him a chance to understand what she was going through and where she was coming from. Maybe he had changed and missed her.

Maybe this opportunity to catch up was just what they needed.

Twenty-Four

THE STUDENT UNION WAS SO EMPTY AND QUIET that Connor could hear the buzz of the fluorescent lights overhead. Having just taken what he could assume was the last final exam being offered on campus for the semester, his plan was to grab a quick sandwich from his favorite deli before heading home for Christmas break.

He paid for his food, taking the bag in his hand, and turned to pick a seat. A few people were scattered throughout the tables, but one couple sitting together caught his eye. He felt his stomach drop, losing his appetite.

Caroline, no. You can't go back to him. Connor ducked into a booth before they could see him. He sat on the edge of his seat, gripping the table, watching her.

Ryan was talking nonstop, that much was obvious. Caroline was listening and nodding her head every now and then. But Connor couldn't get past how sad she looked.

He had never meant to make her fear worse. He had just wanted to help her. But maybe he had moved too fast. Maybe Edison had been too much for her.

He just wished he knew.

Edison had regressed with Caroline's absence. He was back to being fearful of everything and everyone. The walls of his stall were covered with new kick marks. He was going to hurt himself, or someone else, which was why his parents had made the difficult decision to have him euthanized. Tomorrow.

It hadn't been easy, and they had been agonizing over it for weeks. They had tried everything they knew to do to get close to Edison, to touch him, but he didn't let anyone near him. He wouldn't let anyone in.

All he wanted was Caroline.

Connor exhaled with a shaky breath, hating the thought of losing them both. He settled back in his seat, leaving his food untouched, staring at Caroline. He wished he could have a chance to say everything he should've said since he told her he knew about her accident. He'd been rehearsing it in his mind every day since.

An idea popped into his head, something that he should've done sooner. Days ago. He reached into his backpack and pulled out his laptop. It took a couple of minutes to open up and to log in to his email account. He typed Caroline's name into the "to" box and selected her email address as it popped up.

Connor stared at the vertical line flashing on the blank white space in front of him. He closed his eyes, taking a deep breath. *God, please, give me the words.*

His fingers found the keyboard, clicking away as he opened up his heart. He wasn't much of a writer, but he had to at least try. He couldn't give up on her yet.

And he wouldn't until she knew everything he had to say.

Twenty-Five

WIDE AWAKE, CAROLINE STARED AT THE CEILING. She was exhausted, but she was too afraid of the dreams that were waiting for her on the other side. Sitting up, she threw her blankets off her legs and turned on the bedside lamp. She padded across the carpet and sat down at her desk.

She moved the cursor of her laptop, waking it up. A notification dinged as her desktop image loaded, revealing that she had an email.

Connor's name screamed at her from the top of the screen. Her heart pounded in her ears as she moved the little white arrow over to the message. She hesitated to open it, but she knew she needed to see what he had said. Her mouth popped open as soon as she saw how long the email was.

Dear Caroline,

I hope it's okay that I am writing you. You look so sad tonight, and I can't help but feel like it is my fault. I guess I want one more chance to try and fix things. And I guess I should back up and say I'm not stalking you. I just happened to be in the union getting some dinner, and I saw you with Ryan. Whatever happens, or doesn't happen, please, don't get back together with him.

You deserve so much more. But I'll do my
best to keep my opinion on that to myself.

Caroline chuckled under her breath. *No worries there,
Connor.* She hadn't enjoyed her evening with Ryan at all.
He hadn't asked her about anything, not about her classes
or her parents. He had just talked, or bragged, about
himself and about baseball. It had been a waste of time.
She blinked as she found her place on the email and kept
reading.

> Caroline, I'm so sorry for whatever happened
> at the open house that made you even more
> afraid. And I'm sorry if I did the wrong thing
> by not telling you I knew who you were from
> the beginning. I promise you everything I
> did, or didn't do or say, was an attempt to
> help you. You have such a gift with horses...I
> just wanted you to see that.
>
> Horses aside, I wanted to answer my own
> question. I asked you who you were, and
> you told me you didn't know. You are a great
> person. You are a person who has dealt with
> a lot of pain and loss. You are a girl with a
> gift. And most importantly, you are a girl
> God cares about. I've read a few verses
> this week that I wanted to share with you.
> I'm sure you've read them, back before you
> didn't believe.
>
> Matthew 11:28-30: Come to me, all you who
> are weary and burdened, and I will give you
> rest. Take my yoke upon you and learn from
> me, for I am gentle and humble in heart, and

you will find rest for your souls. For my yoke is easy and my burden is light.

Romans 8:28, 38–39: And we know that in all things God works for the good of those who love Him, who have been called according to His purpose... For I am convinced that neither death nor life, neither angels nor demons, neither the present nor the future, nor any powers, neither height nor depth, nor anything else in all creation, will be able to separate us from the love of God that is in Christ Jesus our Lord.

And the last one, Jeremiah 29:11: "For I know the plans I have for you," declares the Lord, "plans to prosper you and not to harm you, plans to give you hope and a future."

I know in the middle of loss, it is hard to believe that He cares. If He cared, He would have kept the bad stuff from happening, right? Believe me, I've struggled with these thoughts myself over Emily. But I've come to understand it doesn't work that way, even if we wish it did.

God is the master planner and creator. He sees an image and a story that we can't even dream of. He can use our pain and our loss, and our doubts, to fulfill His plan. We just have to trust Him. I know this is all easier said than done.

If you hadn't lost horses, you never would have found softball, and I'm sure there are people in your life that you love, that you never would have met without playing the sport. On the other hand, if you hadn't lost softball, you probably wouldn't have met me. And who knows, maybe right now you're wishing you hadn't. But I, for one, am glad you did. Our friendship became really important to me this semester, and even if I never hear from you again, it's something I will never forget or let go of.

I had never told anyone about Emily before, and it was great to finally be able to talk about her, especially to someone who knows that kind of pain. I'll always be thankful to you for that. Maybe that's the end of our story. You came into my life for a season, so I could share Emily's memory, and now you're gone. I hope that's not the end, but again, I don't know God's plan here.

I wish I had the answers for you, but I don't. I believe your gift and your purpose have to do with horses, with Edison. But even if they don't, I need you to know that God does have a purpose for you, that He cares about you, and that you matter to Him.

And that I care about you and that you matter to me, too.

Caroline wiped away the tears from her cheeks. She wanted to believe it. She wanted to believe God still cared about her, but she just didn't know how. She blinked, so she could read the last part.

I feel like I've rattled on here and not made much sense. But I can only hope God does what I can't do.

There's one last thing I have to tell you, even though it kills me to do so. Edison has gotten worse, much worse, since the incident at the open house. We've made the impossible decision to euthanize him tomorrow before he hurts himself, or someone else. He's just too dangerous and unpredictable. It's heartbreaking, and a last resort. I'm not telling you this to make you feel guilty or to make you feel like you need to do anything. I just thought you would want to know.

Regardless of what happens, tomorrow or weeks or months from now, please remember you have a purpose. There is a reason for you being here. And please know, I am always here. You have my number, my email, and you know where I live. I will always be your friend, I am always here if you need me, and I will always be praying for you.

Take care,

Connor

Sad and angry sobs broke free from Caroline's chest. She covered her face with her hands as the tears came down. *Not Edison. No. That poor horse. He doesn't deserve that.*

She forced herself to breathe, focused on getting air in and out of her lungs. Her sobs stopped, leaving behind just a few stray tears. Stumbling to her closet, she opened the door and sat down, reaching in and running her hand over a smooth, wooden box. Her fingers left a trail in the dust coating the lid. She pulled it out, running her thumb over the cold, metal clasp.

The box creaked as she opened it. Tension built up in her stomach as the headline from the Evening Nation jumped out at her from the top of the box's contents: "Caroline Davis Critically Injured in Rotational Fall. Beaus and Ribbons Euthanized." Caroline picked up the article, the paper rattling as her fingers trembled. She saw the picture of her and Beau from their last competition before the accident at the North American Young Riders Championships. They were clearing the Preliminary cross-country fence with a foot to spare, locked on the next jump. They had been the favorite to win the Championships and had been sitting in first after Dressage. But one wrong step before the double log, with a height of three feet, seven inches and an even larger width had caused Beau to hang a leg on the front of the jump, sending them both to the ground. The horse had scrambled, trying to get off Caroline, but his injuries had been too severe. He couldn't get up. Caroline could remember the fear in his eyes, the same eyes she'd seen on Edison.

The next items in the box were letters from riders and trainers all around the country who had been pulling for her as she spent six weeks in the hospital. Her pelvis had been fractured, and she had some other internal injuries. She moved past the letters, to all the ribbons and medals she and Beau had won. Fingering the silky cloth, she could almost hear the applause and cheer of the crowd during a victory lap.

Caroline put the pile of ribbons aside and came to the

last item in the box. To this day, she didn't know who had been kind enough to do this, to save the only part of Beau they could. She gently fingered the braided piece of black and gray tail that was tied together with maroon ribbon, and lifted it from the box. Maroon had been Beau's color. She lifted the tail to her face and inhaled. Even after years of being in that box, it still smelled like her beloved partner.

The touch of his tail and the smell of Beau was too much to take. Caroline found herself sobbing again, crying for the horse she had loved and couldn't save, but also for the girl she had been.

Minutes passed before she felt like she was all cried out. Her eyes were red and raw, and her heart was torn open. Exhausted and trembling, she put the ribbons, the letters, and the article back in the box. She clutched the braided tail to her chest and lay back down, turning off the light.

Caroline fell into a brief and restless sleep. The desperate whinnies of Beau and Edison in her dreams woke her up. Her pillow was damp with a mix of sweat and tears, and her heart was pounding. She rolled over on to her back and stared up at the ceiling. She watched the fan whirling above her head and thought about the part of her secret that no one knew, not even Connor.

That she blamed herself for Beau's death.

If she'd ridden him to that jump differently, or hadn't been trapped under him after he fell, she could have saved him. If she'd put up a stronger fight as the paramedics loaded her into the ambulance, she could have begged the vet to try something, anything, besides putting him down. Or if there was truly nothing that could have been done for him, she could have at least been there to say goodbye. To ask him for forgiveness. And now another horse would lose his life because she was trapped.

She remembered a piece of one of her sporadic, restless dreams: she was galloping toward a jump, the wind rushing past her through the grass and the trees, the red and blond mane brushing against her cheeks as she and the horse set their eyes and hearts onto the fence before them. She was happy, happier than she could remember being since before the wreck.

She tried to go back to sleep, but she couldn't let go of the idea of happiness and Edison. She finally gave up, got dressed, and made her way to her car.

She had one destination in mind.

Twenty-Six

THE LONGING IN CAROLINE'S HEART tangled with the fear in her mind. With shaking hands, she pulled her car over just before the long driveway. Checking in her rearview mirror, she saw tears and terror reflecting from her pale blue eyes. *It's now or never. He needs you.* She blinked back her tears as she pulled her car back on to the road. The sun fought to peak through low-hanging clouds that clung to the tops of the mountains. The few rays that won cast a golden glow over everything they reached. Parking her car, she eased her door shut. Her feet sank into the damp soil, forcing her to slow her steps. She didn't want anyone to know she was there.

Caroline pulled her gray sweatshirt closer to her body, placing the hood over her ponytail to hide her hair and face. She crept her way down the fence line, sneaking her way closer to the smallest barn on the property. It loomed ahead of her. Her body went numb and her heart pounded as she thought about going in, as she remembered the last time she had seen Edison and how terrified and angry he had been. But she knew she had to get to him. She knew she had a job to do. Two futures were at stake.

She managed to go unseen until she reached her chosen destination. She heard the voices of Connor's parents inside the office, just by the entrance. She peered around the corner, wondering if all of this would be in vain. She saw the door to the office was partly closed, so she quickened her pace and slid past. She rushed by without making a sound.

Caroline slowed her steps as she continued down the aisle. She could sense Edison's tension and restlessness from two doors down, forcing her to pause and wonder if she could really handle this.

A hand reached out and touched her shoulder, startling her. She gasped and whirled around, wondering who had discovered her.

"What are you doing here?" Connor whispered.

She read his expression before answering. He wasn't mad at her, didn't seem upset. Just curious. She swallowed back the tears that threatened to fall as she answered. "Connor...I want to believe again. I want to find the purpose God has for me. If it really is Edison, I can't let it happen. I can't let him die without trying. I'm so tired of being trapped."

One tear escaped from her eye and onto her cheek. Connor reached out and wiped it away with his thumb. "I'm glad you came."

"I'm sorry. For disappearing, for not telling you about me. And my accident. I should have. I still want to." Caroline searched his eyes. "But I need to see Edison first."

"You can tell me anything you want to. I'll even give you some fries or something." Connor smiled to lighten the moment. "But you're right. We should see him first."

Together they headed to the stallion's stall. Caroline's breath caught in her throat as she saw how much weight he had lost in the three weeks since the open house. He was tense and his muscles were rigid again. "Oh, Edison," she gasped as more tears threatened to fall.

"I know. It's bad."

Edison squealed and kicked the wall, the door vibrating from his power. He eyed Caroline and Connor, pawing at the ground. Caroline swallowed, focusing on the horse and the happiness she had felt when she was riding him in her one good dream.

Slipping her hand into Connor's, she closed her eyes, trying something she hadn't done in years. *God, I want to believe in You and Your purpose for me. I may never understand why I had to lose Beau, or why I had to get hurt, but You do. I want to try and move past it. I don't want to be trapped. Can you help me? Can You show me what to do?*

When Caroline opened her eyes, she felt more peace than she had in a long time. She looked up at Connor. "Can I go in?"

"Yeah, just please be careful."

"I will be. And you'll be here, right?" Caroline gave Connor a small smile.

He smiled back. "I'm not going anywhere."

Caroline took a deep breath, focusing on Edison. She unlatched the stall door, pulling it open just wide enough for her to sneak in. Edison arched his neck, flattening his ears against his head.

"Hey, boy. You don't need to do that. It's just me. Remember?" Caroline kept her voice low, and kept her eyes down toward the floor, the least threatening place for her gaze. He lowered his head, snorting at her.

Caroline took a few more small steps toward him. His ears relaxed as he blinked at her. "That's a good boy. It's just me. I'm not going to do anything to hurt you, okay?"

When she got close enough to touch him, she reached out, rubbing his shoulder with her knuckles. His muscles twitched, tightening as he arched his neck again. His eyes rolled back at her, the whites of his eyes showing. Fear started to rise in her stomach, and tears stung at her eyes, but she shoved them away. "Please, Edison," she whispered. "I couldn't save Beau, but please, let me save you. I'm sorry I disappeared. It won't happen again. I need you as much as you need me."

Edison flicked his ears as he listened to her. His eyes softened as he recognized her. "There you go, buddy." Caroline murmured to him, petting his shoulder. Edison sighed, and his entire body relaxed. He turned his head and nuzzled Caroline's hair with his nose.

Caroline didn't move a muscle as Edison blew his breath into her face. She inhaled the scent of his sweet breath, smiling through her tears. Reaching up, she ran her fingers through his forelock. She turned, meeting Connor's gaze, and saw tears in his eyes, too.

Connor took slow steps into the stall, stopping behind Caroline. Edison stretched his neck out, taking in his scent, before turning his attention back to Caroline. Connor lifted his hand, placing it over Caroline's, lacing his fingers with hers, intertwining them with Edison's flaxen forelock.

Caroline smiled, looking over her shoulder at Connor. "I think he's going to be okay."

Connor smiled back at her, looking at Edison, then back to her. "I think we all are."

About the Author

ERICA ZABORAC is from Southern Arizona. She earned her bachelor's degree in Animal Science with an Equine Emphasis from the University of Arizona. She earned her master's degree from Southern New Hampshire University in English and Creative Writing.

Erica is a middle school math and science teacher and owns eight horses.

Erica's love for writing began in elementary school. In fifth grade, a poem she wrote was selected for publication. She realized her thoughts and dreams came to life when put down on paper.

Writing remains Erica's first love. *Caroline's Purpose* is her debut novel. She wants to use her gift and love of writing to bring glory to God, and to encourage her readers into a relationship with Him.

Connect with Erica at:

ericazaborac.wordpress.com
facebook.com/ezaboracauthor
instagram.com/ezaborac